Yin-Yang Code

The Drums of Tenkai-Bo

Written by
Warren Chaney
Sho Kosugi

Illustrated by
Shinobu Ohno
Warren Chaney

Library of Congress Cataloguing-in-Publication Data
Chaney, Warren and Kosugi, Sho
Yin–Yang Code – The Drums of Tenkai-Bo
ISBN - 978-0-9990698-5-1 (illustrated perfect binding)

Published by Mindstir Media LLC
45 Lafayette Rd. Suite 181 | North Hampton, NH 03862 | USA
1.800.767.0531 | www.mindstirmedia.com

Written by Warren Chaney and Sho Kosugi
Illustrated by Shinobu Ohno and Warren Chaney
-1st Ed., 316 p. cm.

Summary:

Against his grandfather's wish, an orphaned Japanese student at UCLA returns to his home country following the tragic loss of his close friend and university professor only to discover a malevolent force that aims to take away everything he has left. He discovers that the malicious power seeks an ancient treasure and that he alone holds the key to its recovery.

[1. Fiction. 2. Martial Arts – Fiction. 3. Japanese Culture.
4. Mythology. 5. Treasure. 6. Mystery. 7. History. 8. Art.
9. Conspiracy– Fiction 10. Adventure – Fiction.]

Editors – Dominic Endrinal, Stewart Katz

Printed in the U.S.A.
First edition, April 2017

The text type was set in Bookman Old Style
Book Design by Derek Murphy

MINDSTIR MEDIA

Dedication

This book is gratefully dedicated to the memory of the late Gordon Hessler, who was so helpful in the development of this book. He was a wonderful filmmaker, thinker, and overall great person. We are saddened that he was unable to see the final product that resulted in The Yin–Yang Code – The Drums of Tenkai-Bo, but from "up there" we hope that you are enjoying it.

To quote the line from a famous film, *"Here's to you, Kid!"*

Acknowledgment

The authors are especially indebted to Gordon Hessler and Shane Kosugi, both of whom were a major help with the original story concept. We are also grateful to our attorney, Mike Jackson who was always available for guidance, ideas, and proof reading.

We are especially thankful for all the help that our editors, Dr. Dominic Endrinal and Mr. Stewart Katz, provided. Editing is always a very difficult job, frequently combative and often thankless. With them, it was never contentious and we are extremely thankful for their efforts.

CONTENTS

PREFACE

Before there were adventures of Sinbad, Aladdin, Davy Crockett or Indiana Jones, there was Kūkai, known posthumously as Kōbō-Daishi.

Kūkai was an amazing Japanese Monk who was both a skilled martial artist as well as Japan's most brilliant scholar. Among his many achievements is as the invention of the kana, a syllabary that, in combination with Chinese characters (Kanji), formed the Japanese language as it is written to this day.

Adventurer, engineer, scholar, man of mystery, it is the Kūkai legend that inspires the story you are about to read.

Much of the wonderful Japanese culture is woven into the fabric of the adventure before you. We sincerely hope that you enjoy it and that perhaps will one day, you will take a trip to the enchanted land of the rising sun.

Warren Chaney and Sho Kosugi

Into the Storm

INTO THE STORM
Chapter One

"Do not seek to follow in the footsteps of the men of old; instead, seek what they sought."

Kukai – 832 CE

J AGGED STREAKS OF LIGHTNING explode across a tempestuous July sky, illuminating a Japanese junk craft trapped in a Sea of Japan's violent typhoon squall. Roaring waves of ocean water repeatedly swamp the rugged wooden decks as hardened sailors valiantly heave cargo overboard in an attempt to lighten the load of the endangered ship.

The year is 804 AD, and the craft, one of four ships in a Japanese convoy, travels to China carrying valuable trading goods and passengers. The intensity of the violent storm, however, threatens the destination of both.

Waves sweep the bow making the crew's task increasingly difficult. Meanwhile, other deckhands endeavor to secure running backstay lines binding the jibs and main sheets to prevent their being ripped from the ship's planking.

Then, all of sudden, a series of sails attached to the mizzen and foremast collapse under a blustery gale of wind, sending them crashing against the foremast. The wooden structure strains under the extra load and begins to crack.

Gonzo, an older Japanese seaman in his late fifties hears the splintering wood and rushes toward a mass of rigging which tugs against the upper stays of the foremast. He knows the ship will be lost if the foremast snaps in a storm of this magnitude; and therefore loses no time making his way toward the pending calamity. Glancing upward, he sees a single rope traps the sails, binding them to the mast and rendering their release impossible without toppling the entire wooden beam.

The ship heels wildly, rolling to the starboard side under pressure from the wind and collapsed rigging. If it continues to tilt, the violent ocean water may just as well swamp the hull, which would carry it under the waves. The only chance is to change the ship's center of gravity, but the crew is too scattered, and there is not much time to gather them all at once.

The sailor scrambles up and over the mixed weave of sail, sheets, and line. He makes his way to the top, and quickly cuts the forestay to release the bulk of unstable weight before a crosstree whips loose and strikes the sailor and sends him plunging toward the deck.

With a controlled sense of immediacy, the falling seaman grasps one of the trailing lines and breaks his fall, but his leg becomes entangled in a rope crinkle. A swinging beam strikes him across the body, extending his fall; his ensnared leg catches the rope and dangles him helplessly from the furling of the mainsail.

Deck water sweeps over the ship planking past a sturdy teakwood hatch that leads to the craft's quarterdeck cabin. The access-way bursts open, and an athletic man, about thirty-one years old and dressed in a black colored priestly robe, storms through the enclosure. Five other priests follow him but they cower near the hatch, whereas the first priest steps boldly into the storm. His keen dark eyes, close- shaven head, and black-robed priestly attire set him apart in this otherwise ethereal setting. The man is Kukai, a superiorly trained Japanese monk. Though young, he is already acknowledged as one of Japan's emerging intellects and philosophers.

Kukai surveys the situation, and glancing across the ship's bow, spots the seaman helplessly suspended from the masthead rigging. The monk quickly throws off his robe and leaps into the air, away from the quarterdeck.

His strong hands grasp one of the long-trailing lines attached to the mainmast, and he swings in a log arch from the ship's stern. Midway, he quickly transfers to another line that carries him toward the foremast. Then a heavy blast of wind suddenly interrupts his swing and lifts him even higher, up and away from the ship. The line slips from his grasp while his body arches higher because of the wind, and then drops toward the deck.

Kukai quickly retrieves a short but wide Japanese dagger, called a *tantō*, from his waistband and places it between his teeth; he spins into a headlong dive toward a billowing mainsail. Both hands grasp the handle on his downward flight, and as he nears the sail, plunges it into the linen fabric. The dagger cuts through the fabric which helps slow Kukai's descent toward the trapped Japanese sailor. As he approaches the sailor, he yanks the blade from the sail with one hand and grabs another ship's line with the other. The line carries the monk past the hanging man, and while it does so, Kukai swings his blade and slashes the mooring that ensnares its victim.

The freed sailor grips a shroud and is now safely inverted as the tangled web of sails tumble to the deck below where other monks are clinging to the ship's ropes and boarding while they cringe in ominous fear.

Kukai follows the falling sails, sliding down his

rope and landing on his feet. As he strikes the deck, the ship leans violently to one side.

A second gust of heavy wind slams against the ship and causes it to tilt to its starboard side. Waves of storm-water pour over the ship and threaten to sink it. Lightning strikes the masthead, setting it on fire, although the rolling water immediately extinguishes the blaze. Just when sinking seems inevitable, the ship slopes to its portside, causing storm waves to slam against the bulkhead and tilt the craft further into the water.

The screaming men and cringing monks Sensing their end is near, the screaming men and cringing monks grasp at anything solid to keep them from being thrown into the icy-cold and dark ocean waters.

Although completely aware of the danger at hand, Kukai maintains his composure as he braces against a masthead. He is unfazed by the falling debris and whipping sail lines. He stares straight into the heart of the storm and lightning and soon begins chanting a *sūtra*, starting low but increasing in intensity, *"Om amogha vairocana maha-mudra mani padma jvaia pravataya hun."*

A lightning bolt strikes a sail runner above Kukai's head. He does not budge even though the fall wood structure slams against him.

The experienced crewmembers know their fate, accept it even. This is the end. Still, despite everything, Kukai repeats the chant, *"Om amogha vairocana maha-mudra mani padma jvaia pravataya hun!"*

One of the heavier lines of the ship smacks him across the face and draws blood. But Kukai remains unfazed.

KUKAI MAINTAINS HIS SERENITY IN THE FACE OF A VIOLENT STORM IN THE SEA OF JAPAN.

A few of the men begin to scream ear-piercing nightmarish sounds of fear. Unable to hold on, some of the men slip into the black depths of the ocean as the ship threatens to capsize. Intense waves crash against Kukai, but he undauntedly maintains the haunting chant.

Suddenly, the ship stops, impossibly balanced on its side. The experienced and stunned seamen watch as the vessel slowly begins to right itself. What they see is beyond their comprehension. The storm still rages all around them; but they feel as if the ship is somehow protected. Kukai continues chanting, now his voice rising above the storm.

Once the ship has righted, lightning flashes abruptly diminish, the bolts of thunder even fade. The tumultuous sprays vanish, and the waters smoothen until all that is left is a silence, a quiet void of any turbulence or sound, save the silent splashing of soft waves against the hull.

The men climb down from their perches and gather around the monk; and as insecure as they are, remain some safe distance away. The Japanese seaman who has been saved, drops to the deck. He shakes rather fearfully, not so much because of the storm as from what he has just witnessed. The other monks, still cowering in the shadows of the quarterdeck, gradually stand, equally awestruck at what they have beheld.

The chant stops as Kukai inhales sharply and slowly raises his head. The seamen who have lived swear to their grave that a faint light shines from their savior's eyes before it vanishes very much like the storm.

KUKAI – SCHOLAR, ENGINEER, AND MARTIAL ARTIST

THE CRYPTIC MANTRA
Chapter Two

AN ARTFULLY DRAWN PROJECTED image of Kukai fades and the darkened classroom brightens up as Dr. Ben Thompson walks from the back of his 135-student classroom toward a podium located to the right of the screen. The professor is in his early forties, although he appears much older.

Dr. Thompson's neatly brushed mop of brown hair sits atop a high forehead, below which is a set of keenly intelligent-dark-hazel eyes. His weathered face tells many years of outdoors exposure. He is overweight, paunchy, and walks with a slight stoop to his shoulders. Prof. Thompson's body projects the image of one who has spent more time thinking than moving.

The professor pauses to observe casually a poster that has been on his classroom wall: an athletic poster, a football team of the University of California, Los Angeles. Prof. Thompson barely notices it as he continues his lecture on Japanese history and culture class.

"Kukai, also known as Kōbō-Daishi, was on his way to China to study both the profound and exotic Buddhism under Master Hui-kuo, supreme leader of the movement at the time. From age nineteen to thirty he had already studied Taoism, Buddhism, Confucianism, and the Analects of Confucius."

A chubby-faced student raises his hand and asks as Dr. Thompson points to him, "What are analects?"

"Analects are a collection of sayings and ideas attributed to Confucius and his followers," replies Prof. Thompson, who moves to one side of his podium, and then continues. "Anyway, at the age of 31, Kukai was determined to go to China to study. He had to do it then because the next 17th Japanese Envoy to China's Tang Dynasty would be some thirty years later."

A young female teen in a blue-plaid shirt raises her hand and when acknowledged by the professor asks, "How did he manage to get on the travel list?"

Prof. Thompson laughs and says, "Thank you, Miss Dunn. Your question is at a most opportune time."

The class laughs and as the laughter subsides, the professor continues. "Kukai's task was nearly insurmountable. It cost a small fortune, which he was able to raise from sponsors, patrons, investors, brothers-in-law . . ."

The class cannot help it and laughs again.

"All of this had to happen. On top of that, however, Kukai had to pass a tough government exam to become a certified priest under the Imperial Court, along with an immense advanced physical training that was part of the requirement. But he was smart and he got it all done so that by 804 AD, he was already an official member of the 16th Japanese Envoy to Tang Dynasty and was on his way to China."

"Kukai's vessel and another craft were spared

in the storm. The remaining two ships were lost at sea, with   hundreds of lives in them."

Prof. Thompson yanks the UCLA football themed poster from the wall and resumes his lecture.

"Kukai expected to spend twenty years studying in China, but he was so brilliant that within a few short months, he received the final initiation and became a master of esoteric or mystical Buddhism. He then returned to Japan and developed into the legend that he is today. It is a fact that he studied abroad to seek the Way. He went empty-handed, but returned fully-equipped." The class laughs at Prof. Thompson's attempt to inject humor.

"But make no mistake," continues the professor. "Kukai returned to Japan after spending only two years in China. Most of those who went for this kind of study had to stay twenty or thirty years. So, Kukai's feat was unheard of then in China and in Japan."

Jun raises her hand.

"Yes, Ms. Lee."

"Dr. Thompson, I don't understand. Wouldn't Kukai's quick return be seen as a disgrace?"

"Not at all. First, and foremost, Master Hui-kuo had predicted that Kukai would visit him and study under his supervision. Then the master chose the best seven; that is seven out of one thousand disciples. He taught them everything he knew about Esoteric Buddhism."

"And they learned it all?" Michael asks incredulously.

"Nope, only one of them did," answers Prof.

Thompson as he moves closer to the students. "That one was Kukai. Before Hui-kuo died, he had appointed Kukai the 8th Esoteric Buddhism, Shingon Sect Successor in China."

Jun raises her hand and delivers her question right off the bat. "Didn't he get flak for that? I mean, I read there were native Chinese who had studied for decades . . ."

"Indeed, he did. Many thought they should have been chosen, but that didn't happen. The torch had been passed to Kukai. When and after all of this happened, the rumor mill started."

"Such as what, Professor?" inquires Jose.

"There was a rumor that the Imperial Court had requested Kukai's return. The gossip's rationale was that to have him otherwise returned so quickly would have resulted in punishment and death."

"Was the story true?" asks Steve Chan, a handsome, young Chinese who, as a child, had immigrated to the U.S. with his parents.

"If it was," Prof. Thompson answers with a smile, "nobody knew the reason except Kukai himself and the Emperor."

"What do you think, Professor?" Steve seriously asks.

"Kukai was smart, extremely intelligent. He did thirty years of work in two years. You must think of him as the Japanese counterpart of Italy's Leonardo Da Vinci. There was no one like him in history. Kukai was extraordinarily diverse. He was a Japanese monk, civil engineer, scholar, poet, and artist. He was the founder of the Shingon or "True Word" school of Esoteric Buddhism," Dr.

Thompson further explains. Smiling, he turns to his class and asks in Japanese, *"Kare wa hoka ni nani o shimashita ka?"*

A pregnant pause ensues as the young students try to process the Japanese language.

"We are learning to speak Japanese in this class, are we not?" inquires the professor.

"Hai," answers a student from the third row at the back. *"Kare wa sakka demo arimashita."*

The student is sandy-haired William Strong, a former Harvard graduate who has enrolled in UCLA's Asian culture program. He smiles, confident that his Japanese response is right on.

"Thank you, Mr. Strong," replies Prof. Thompson. "My question was, 'What else did Kukai do?' and William's answer was, 'Kukai was a writer,' and he is correct."

William smiles and glances over to his fellow student, Jun Lee, an attractive exchange-student from South Korea.

"Mr. Strong is correct, as far as he goes. However, he doesn't go far enough."

William turns back to Prof. Thompson, uncertain that he may have gotten part of his answer incorrect.

"For the Japanese," continues the professor, "Kukai invented their writing. When he returned from his studies in China, he took forty-eight 'letters' from the Chinese characters; then simplified and adapted them to form a phonetic script that has since been in use in writing today. As I've said, Kukai was a very brilliant man."

STEVE CHAN, A HANDSOME, YOUNG CHINESE WHO, AS A CHILD, HAD IMMIGRATED TO THE U.S. WITH HIS PARENTS.

William Strong smiles broadly, relieved that he is not completely wrong.

"Kukai quickly became the acknowledged master of mysticism in Japan, with his fame reaching China and spreading even farther," says the professor.

"What was the chant you had him doing, Doctor?" asks Steve.

"The Guang Ming Mantra," Prof. Thompson quickly replies. "It is one of the enlightening hymns, or chants, from the Shingon-sect as well as Shugendo."

Thompson turns his attention to a young blonde co-ed, Violet Carr, whose hazel eyes twinkle, happy for the kind attention.

"And we have learned that Shugendo is what, Ms. Carr?"

Smiling broadly, Violet replies, "It's a philosophy for living simply and completely in a complicated and confusing world."

"Yes, but it is a little more than a philosophy," adds the professor. "Anything more, Mr. Rodriguez?"

Jose Rodriguez, Violet's boyfriend, sits adjacent to her. He does not expect to be addressed the question but quickly sums up a response.

"Well, Shugendo involves an awakening that comes about through an understanding of the relationship between humanity and nature," retorts Jose

"And what is involved in its learning then?" probes Prof. Thompson.

"The training is centered on a Spartan-like, mountain-dwelling, physical-and-mental practice that involves continuing hardships," Jose says as a rejoinder.

"Correct, Mr. Rodriquez," says the professor, but now addresses his rather sizable class. "But make no mistake; Shugendo is much more than a religion. It's a creed, a strict way of thinking which its practitioners believe will make our planet a better place to live."

Prof. Thompson briefly pauses as though he is lost in thought for a moment. Shortly he regains himself and resumes his lecture.

"For the superior practitioner pursuing Shugendo, however, the benefits produced go far beyond the power of words to describe. Many consider Shugendo to be the only path toward acquiring divine mystical power. As Mr. Rodriguez, has pointed out to us, Shugendo is accomplished only through continuous practice and spiritual application."

Michael Wood, a handsome young black student, dressed in a dark-blue, white-trimmed, short-sleeved shirt and dungarees, sits with Jose and Violet, raises his hand.

Prof. Thompson starts to call on him, but before he can, Michael already has eagerly mouthed his question, "Was Kukai the originator of Shugendo?"

"There is little doubt that Kukai contributed to its development, but the basis of Shugendo extends backward, more than 1,300 years, to a much earlier religious belief system in Japan. Its disciples, the Yamabushi, strive to divest themselves of all human blemishes toward purification," Prof. Thompson further explains. "But back to your question, Mr. Wood. The one person responsible for Shugendo, as it is today, is En no Ozunu."

"Who is that, Professor?" Jun asks for clarification.

Prof. Thompson activates his remote control to darken the room. Immediately, a projected image of En no Ozunu fills the screen and shows him to be a stout, ceremoniously-robed warrior with white, shoulder-length hair, and a pointed *yagi-hige*-style mustache and beard.

"Japan's most celebrated holy man and Father of Shugendo is En no Ozunu, sometimes called En no Gyōja. He was a Japanese aesthetic, a mystic, or magician, if you will. Ozunu was widely acclaimed for his sorcery, envied for his power, and was once falsely accused of the witchcraft of delusion. Thus, an ancient court banished him; but he transcended those who sentenced him. They are now forgotten, but Ozunu is the one who is remembered," Prof. Thompson keeps expounding.

"En no Ozunu predated Kukai who was born more than a hundred years later. Ozunu died in 706 AD, and Kukai in 835 AD. Although they lived in separate times, both had much in common with the mystical world of spiritualism. Shugendo today incorporates both their thinking and contributions. Legend has it that Kukai did not die but entered into an eternal *samadhi* and is still alive on Mount Koya, awaiting the appearance of Maitreya, the future Buddha."

Prof. Thompson briefly pauses the film image and interjects, "It might interest you to know that there were two monks who had carted for more than two miles Kukai's meals for over twelve centuries."

"Why is that, Dr. Thompson?" queries Michael Woods.

"They had to bring the food from a specially anointed Yuina priest whose responsibility was the preparation of Kukai's food. Over the course of history, this special priest had served without stopping, not even for a single day, regardless of fires and earthquakes; even two World Wars!" adds Prof. Thompson. "Let me point out to all of you that even Ozunu's spirit is said to be alive in the Tsurugi mountain regions or those of Marozan."

"Are there any Shugendo monks left in Japan?" asks William.

"Oh, yes, indeed, very much so!" replies the professor. "Today, a Shugendo monk, called a Shugenja, trains much the same way as at the time of Ozunu. Here, let me show you."

The screen brightens again to show two monks dressed in the ancient orange linen and flax robes and clothing of their forebears. Each wears a small black round box called a *tokin*, tied to the foreheads. The monks play trumpet conches, which are spiraled tropical marine shells used to call other monks and priests climbing the mountain and training as they proceed.

The screen image shifts to Shugenja who are sitting under a snow-crested waterfall while icy water pours over their bodies, as a test of their endurance.

Once more, the images change to show a beautiful, if not extravagant, temple. One of the clips display five hundred separate statues affixed to one wall of the temple.

"This is the beautiful Zentsu-ji Temple that marks Kukai's birthplace. The temple has undergone several reconstructions over time and is now very, very old. Kukai built it himself in 807 AD. It is an important stopping place for the eighty-eight-temple pilgrimage."

"Eighty-what, Doctor?" asks a tanned male student from the back row.

"Eighty-eight," Dr. Thompson replies. "Kukai created not just a path to enlightenment, but a literal track or course that is meant to be traveled spiritually and physically. This Kukai pilgrimage serves as a central visiting point by hundreds of thousands of people worldwide, all seeking guidance in this very troubled world. The Zentsu-ji Temple is a significant site and has great spiritual value like that of the Shingon-sect and the Shugenja."

The professor steps in front of the video projector the pulsating light of which falls across his face and body, thus giving him a rather strange aura.

"Would you care to hear another mantra?" Prof. Thompson asks the whole class.

Michal Wood is the first to say yes, followed closely by Jose, Steve, and William. Others in the class trail them in agreement as well.

The professor transitions the screen to another video of a lone monk sitting before a fire in a small cave. He remains still and immobile and bows before the flame; but as the camera pushes forward, the monk unexpectedly lifts his head. His flashing eyes stare directly into the eyes of his viewing audience. Several in the classroom are caught off guard and do not anticipate the sudden move. Short gasps reverberate through the entire lecture hall.

As the monk's lips move, the chamber fills with the hollow sound of his melancholy chanting mantra, *"Rin, Pyo, Toh, Sha, Kai, Jin, Retsu, Zai, Zen."*

IN ANOTHER AREA, AS dark as the fire-lit cave of the Shugendo monk, a black-draped Shugenja sits before a similar fire. His body blends with the shadows around him, with his closed eyes solely giving contrast to the darkness of the environment.

The monk's chant echoes throughout the cavern, while the Shugenja sits unmoved and unemotional. He listens as though there is a connection between him and the monk, yet he is silent and motionless.

As the mantra begins to repeat itself, the eyes of the Shugenja open. They are as dark as the cavern and as motionless as his body. Then, unexpectedly, the black- masked figure begins to chant in consonance with the Shugenja, *"namaH sarvatahaagatebhyaH . . ."*

"THE MANTRA YOU HEAR is that of the Nine Levels of Power," says Prof. Thompson. "The

Shugenja trained through deprivation and hardship and learned how to control their minds and the minds of others through a power called *Jumon.*"

"I've heard that once before, Dr. Thompson!" exclaims Steve Chan. "It was used by the Ninja long ago."

"Some historians believe that the Shugenja were ancestors of the Ninja because they do have some history in common."

"Such as what, Professor?" prods Steve.

"In Japan, around the early 7th century, the first Ninja appeared. They used various infiltration tactics, targeted assassinations, guerrilla warfare, and so on."

"These were the Ninja?" asks Jose.

Prof. Thompson smiles, "At the time the Ninja weren't called Ninja."

"I thought they've always been called Ninja," Michael is heard saying.

"You've been watching too many movies, Mr. Wood. No, they were called the "Shinobi." Make no mistake, class. The Ninja were feared as were the Shugenja. Like them, the Ninja trained very hard physically and mentally. In Japanese history, they show up in many of the same locations such as the Kinki District in Japan. In fact, they appear wherever the ancient Ninja training occurs . . ."

"The Dojo!" exclaims Michael.

"Yes," says Thompson. "The Dojo. They were wherever those in Japan worshiped and enshrined En No Ozunu. But today, the Shugenja are peaceful and their spells are seldom used."

Without warning, the mantra from the video

abruptly develops an echo and, unexpectedly, the chant from the Ninja joins in concert with the monk's voice from the projector's speakers. Suddenly, haunting sounds of drumbeats, like those of the Taiko, join and mix with the chants; thus, creating a surreal experience.

Everyone strains to locate the source of the new sounds that seemingly emanate from everywhere but comes from nowhere.

The image begins to flare and enlarge and, without notice, engulfs the screen. Concurrently, the images on the screen splutter and break up. Shots of strangely lit monks now appear, then vanish, and then suddenly the "chant from nowhere" becomes louder and now surrounds the students as it reverberates throughout the classroom.

Many in the class scream, with a few others holding their breath. Then, as though materializing from the screen, a monk in a black-lacquered cup strapped to his forehead appears. His back is what the viewers see while he speaks to another monk. They speak in Japanese, but their voices are hollow and warped-sounding.

Raising her hand, Jun asks, "What are they saying?"

The monk facing the students grows increasingly furious, and he and the other man both become noticeably more disturbed. While the camera moves closer to the monk, all the pixilated images begin to form a horrific distortion of his face. The drums are now unbearably loud.

Suddenly, the overhead video projector explodes, followed by Violet's long-piercing scream. Something has gone wrong; quite terribly wrong!

RAISING HER HAND, JUN ASKS, "WHAT ARE THEY SAYING?"

DAIKI IKE

DAIKI
Chapter Three

VIOLET'S SCREAM STARTLES THE others. Jun involuntarily grabs Steve's arm while William nervously sits straight up in his chair.

With the smoke pouring from the projector, the haunting duo of chants continues to reverberate and repeat throughout the room.

The students in the classroom begin placing their hands over their ears. One chant, *"Rin, Pyo, Toh* --------,*"* obviously comes from the projector's speaker system, but the other one, *"namah samanta vajraaNaaM----,"* surrounds everyone as if it is recited individually and directly in each student's ear.

Prof. Thompson is visibly disturbed, and the students even more frightened. Although the projector seems damaged, the now-distorted and weirdly pixilated images continue to display on the screen.

No sooner has the eerie chanting ended than the images vanish and replaced by the earlier Shikoku temple sequences that are a part of Prof. Thompson's lecture.

The highly agitated professor throws his remote at the overhead projector and slams his fist against the projector's wall-mounted power- switch, abruptly cutting off the projected imagery.

"Damn it all! Damn it!" mutters Prof. Thompson.

The class remains silent, somewhat stunned at what has just occurred and by total display of anger by the professor.

Prof. Thompson catches himself, recovers, and half smiles. Then he says, "Must be the projector; but, frankly, it's just too strange . . . okay, class, enough for today!"

Nervous laughter erupts from the students and fills the room.

"That's computer for you, guys," continues Prof. Thompson. "You never know!"

In her effort to recover her composure, Violet nervously places her hand to her chin. Jose simply stares at the blank screen and tries to fathom what has just happened.

IN HER EFFORT TO RECOVER HER COMPOSURE, VIOLET NERVOUSLY PLACES HER HAND TO HER CHIN.

Sitting on the row below Violet and Jose, William jots his observations down in his spiral-bound notebook. The other students, although free to go, remain at their seat.

"Well, I can teach for another hour, or you may call it a day," says Prof. Thompson. "Are you really asking for more?"

The students laugh and then gather their books, ready to leave.

"Don't forget your homework or your papers for next Tuesday. They're due then," remarks Prof. Thompson, getting ready to leave and turning off the lights in the hall.

Most students exit the classroom, but Steve Chan joins Jun Lee, Michael Wood, Jose Rodriguez, and Violet Carr who all are huddled together and still talking by the door. William Strong packs a notebook and his laptop into his dark leather-shoulder bag and then joins the group. From their affable conversation, it is obvious that they are all friends.

"Hey, let's grab a drink at the Student Center before we head out," suggests Steve.

"Works for me," replies William.

"Not me," says Michael. "I have a workout to go to."

"Yeah, yeah. Mr. Antisocial there," teases Jun.

Michael laughs, "Catch you later."

As Michael leaves for the gym, Steve laughingly jokes, "He thinks he's the world's next Bruce Lee."

"Is that Bruce Lee spelled with an 'L' and two 'e's, or is it an 'L' followed by an 'i'?" asks Jun.

"Same thing, huh!" jokes Jose. "Michael

doesn't care whether he's Bruce Lee or Jet Li. He just wants to be in the movies."

"Yeah," laughs Violet. "Any day now, I expect to see him leap out of a tree in a Ninja outfit. You know, like that actor...uh, what's his name, that one who did all the Ninja film?"

"Never mind," quips Jose. "We know what you mean; come on, let's get to the student center. All this talking has made me thirsty."

They stroll away, laughing, and talking.

TWO-STORY APARTMENTS HAVE gradually overwhelmed South Elm Street. It was once a street of family homes but in response to a growing and encroaching university, some of the dwellings have expanded to become boarding houses for those students at nearby UCLA. One of the lodgings at 501 South Elm is an early 1940s faded-blue clapboard structure, where there is a small garden in front surrounded by a white-picket fence.

Mrs. Mae Farmer, an elderly kind widow and landlady to four college students, kneels before her carefully spaced plants, pulling weeds, and hand-spading the mulch. She is in her 70s, but is very alert and active. This time around, she quietly sings to herself refrains of an old hymn, *Blessed Assurance*, while she adds several spoonsful of fertilizer to her azaleas.

From behind the house, a young Asian man pushes a wheelbarrow full of fresh mulch. He hears Mrs. Farmer's singing and stops to listen. The young man is Daiki Ike, a Japanese student who, as a child, came to the United States through his grandfather's decision. Like others in the boarding house, he is also a UCLA student. He's dressed in faded jeans and a patterned blue shirt.

"Here you go, Mrs. Farmer," says the young man, "another load of mulch for you. This should be the last one."

"Thank you very much, Daiki," the woman says warmly. "In this heat, carrying all these loads would have been too much for me. I do appreciate your help, young man."

"Think nothing of it, Mrs. Farmer. Glad to be of help," says Daiki while turning over the wheelbarrow to get its contents closer to Mrs. Farmer.

"Anything else I can do for you?"

"No, no, you've done quite enough," replies Mrs. Farmer. "You have to leave a few things for me to do, or I won't get my exercise. Speaking of which, my oranges are ripening now, I'll get us one."

The woman stands, looking up at an orange tree bearing fruit, but higher on the limbs than she can reach.

"On second thought, I'll need to get my ladder."

"Wait a minute, Mrs. Farmer," says Daiki. "Maybe I can do this."

From his pants pocket, Daiki removes a yo-yo of a rather ornate design. Engraved on its heavy-metal surface is the Japanese symbol depicting two complementary forces that make up all aspects of life--the Yin-Yang. Unlike a regular yo-yo, this one sports a long metallic string with a loop at one end. Daiki inserts his figure into the loop and lets the metal disc drop once before rewinding it. Before it reaches his hand, his arm shoots forward and sends the yo-yo upward. The disc strikes an orange; but before it can fall, the yo-yo spins around Daiki's wrists and returns upward, striking a second orange that falls.

The young Japanese uses his free hand to catch the first orange and flips it to the hand with the yo-yo, and catches the second one.

The yo-yo drops, catches on the metallic cord, and spins to Daiki's hand, joining the orange that is already there.

"Here you go, Mrs. Farmer," says Daiki, handing her an orange.

"That was some exhibition, young man. You never cease to amaze me."

Daiki laughs as he spins the yo-yo back into his hand and side-pocket, after which he lifts the wheelbarrow to carry and stash it away.

"I'll just put this back in the shed for you, Mrs. Farmer."

"Oh, I can do that," says the landlady.

"No trouble. My bike is back there anyway and I need to wheel over to the library. I have some work to do on a paper that's due Friday."

"Well, you be careful on that bike, Daiki. It'll be

dark soon and some of these college kids learned to drive watching *Jeopardy* on television. Besides, they all text constantly while they drive. Land's sake. I've never seen so many moving thumbs in my life!"

Daiki, who was just checking a text message on his cell phone, quickly puts it away as Mrs. Farmer looks up at him.

"Yes, Ma'am, I'll be careful. I'll be going now."

A short time later, Daiki, carrying a satchel on his back, pedals his way to the library when he hears a familiar voice.

"Daiki! Daiki!" shouts a very attractive girl from across the street. Four others, Steve, William, Violet, and Jose, accompany her.

"Hi, Jun," says Daiki who crosses to the other side of the street and glides his bike to a halt.

"Listen, drop what you're doing. You're coming to my sorority. We're having a party. It's a big one."

"I'd like to, but I can't make it."

"But you have to," pleaded Jun. "Everybody will be there."

"I have a paper due; I can't put it off."

"Okay, you're off the hook on this one, but you must make the one on Saturday night, please?"

Daiki shrugs noncommittally as he pulls away on his bike.

"That's a promise then," shouts Jun. "See you there!"

The biker half-turns his head and with a slight smile and brief nod disappears down the street.

"He's a loner, that one," says Steve.

"Little wonder," replies Jun. "You don't know what he's been through."

"She's right," adds Violet. "Lay off him, Steve. At least you've got your mom and dad. Daiki lost his. Only person left is his grandfather and he never sees him."

"Umm, okay ladies. Maybe it's for the better," says Steve while circling his arm around Jun's waist. "No sharing. Now I'll have you to myself."

Jun smiles politely as she pushes Steve's arm away. The expression on her face shows that she is troubled.

The group moves on, passes through a series of large oak trees along the darker portion of the poorly lit street.

All of a sudden, a hooded man wearing Ninja headgear swings upside down from one of the branches.

Violet screams hysterically.

"Juuumon!" cries the Ninja in a hollow voice. "I am in control of your minnnndddd!"

"I knew it. I just knew it," mumbles Jun.

From Violet's first scream, Jose loses no time. He quickly grabs the hanging man and slams him to the ground.

"It's me, Jose. It's me," yelps the fallen figure.

"Knock it off, Michael," shouts Jun as Jose rips the headgear from the prone figure's head, revealing that it is indeed, Michael Wood, the would-be Bruce Lee.

Jun turns to the group, but they are all laughing now. Jose extends his hand and helps Michael up to stand.

Michael dusts himself off, then laughs, and joins his friends as they saunter off toward the party.

DAIKI TAKES A SHORTCUT to the university, cycles briskly through a dark, derelict commercial neighborhood. The economy has experienced bad times and the locked doors with iron gates and boarded up windows, all but reflect it.

Unexpectedly, a dull sound like a popping balloon signals that a tire has just blown. Daiki's bike swerves fiercely to the left, confirming his suspicion. The rear wheel sparks as the steel rim grinds against the concrete pavement. The bicycle tilts toward the street, but Daiki manages to dismount without falling.

The young Japanese man looks around his surroundings, where garbage is strewn everywhere along the street and long graffiti adorns the rows of buildings and torn pavements. The neighborhood has seen the worst of a faltering economy, and its dim infrequent lighting serves as testimony. Daiki quickly wheels his bike to a sidewalk, stops in front of a closed boarded-up Mom and Pop store. Without losing time, Daiki takes off his satchel and flips his bike upside down. He pulls out a small repair kit from the pack and quickly removes the blown front tire.

"Thank goodness it wasn't the back tire," mumbles Daiki to himself as he extracts a nail from the rubber tire. "This would take a lot longer if I had to mess with the chain-drive and all."

Using a small tire-iron to wedge the tire from the rim, Daiki separates the two and takes out the bike's inner tube to find the puncture hole. He opens a tube of tire glue and spreads a thick gooey substance across the punctured surface. He is about to place a fabric patch over it when he is interrupted by a harsh voice.

"You need help, Chink?"

Daiki spins around and notices a young hoodlum in his early twenties standing nearby. He wears a typical outfit that most L.A. gangbangers wear: a tight-cut dingy white-tank top that purposely exposes his muscular-tattooed arms. Long, dirty hair hangs over his ears onto his shoulders.

"I can manage. Thanks," responds Daiki.

The roughneck, tossing his head to one side in an attempt to shift his hair, steps closer, stops by Daiki's satchel that sits on the curb. He studies it as though deciding which contents he wants to remove.

"Oh, you gonna' need help, Chink. You gonna' need help real bad."

Daiki stands to face the man, but then notices that two more thugs have joined the first gangbanger who has drawn a weapon and now points a cheap 38' caliber pistol at him. The other two have pulled knives from their belts. The thug with the gun continues to watch his victim, reaches into Daiki's satchel and yanks a couple of books from the bag, which he proceeds to pitch to the ground. He extends his hand inside the bag once more, but while doing so shifts his eyes from his prey to the perceived loot.

Daiki seizes the moment of distraction and before the thug realizes what is happening, Daiki already has drawn the metal yo-yo from his pocket.

Were it not for its dangerously strange appearance, anybody would think of Daiki's yo-yo simply as a mere yo-yo. In fact, that is precisely what Daiki's attackers believe it is.

One hoodlum, a heavy-set thug whose overly tight shirt exposes a swatch of hairy stomach, mockingly laughs and says, "He's gonna' yo-yo us to death, Max."

"That's just great, 'cause I'm puttin' this Chink down. Now!" replies the gunman.

The gunman instinctively fires his weapon toward Daiki, but his target is no longer there. In that split-second of distraction, Daiki has shifted positions and holds onto one end of his yo-yo by its stout metal cord, and hurls it toward his attacker. The weapon unfurls from its cord, creating a shrill whistling sound as it spins ever more rapidly toward the gunman. The thug cannot move fast enough to avoid the object that crashes against his shoulder, smashing the bone.

The gangster screams in agony, clutches his arm, and drops to the pavement on his knees. He shrieks in even more pain as Daiki snaps the cord, smacking the thug in the head with the heavy metal object before it travels back to its sender's hand.

DAIKI'S WEAPON UNFURLS FROM ITS CHORD, CREATING A SHRILL, WHISTLING SOUND AS IT SPINS EVER MORE RAPIDLY TOWARD THE GUNMAN.

One hoodlum, frightened at seeing his leader go down so easily, lags behind his other friend who rushes headlong into the attack.

The headlong attacker raises his knife-arm to strike, but the loud-pitched whistle of the yo-yo signals it is borne in the air again. The yo-yo strikes the hood's upraised arm, cracks the wrist, bringing intensely awful pain, followed by more agonizing scream.

The last attacker, even though unnerved at what has transpired, saunters toward Daiki. The knife the thug wields starts its downward thrust, but as the blade reaches the point where Daiki is standing, it slices through empty air.

The forward momentum forces the gangster's body to pitch headlong toward the pavement, but before hitting the pavement, Daiki has already stepped to one side, angles his body, and delivers a solid kick to the thug's head.

The sight of three men lying on the sidewalk and screaming in agony would be funny given the circumstances, but for the fact that there are other street-gang members who arrive from various alleyways and side streets. They have heard their comrades' cries and have come to answer their call.

Daiki steps away from the thugs lying on the street and faces the approaching throng of gangsters. He takes careful notes of the number of assailants: about twelve, maybe fourteen. "Too many too soon," he thinks as he positions himself with his back to one of the storefronts, and hopes not to be surrounded by the rushing bunch of hoodlums.

As though of one mind, the goons run directly toward Daiki who hurls his weapon that rapidly takes down two of the gangsters, striking one in the thigh and the other in the hip. He discovers quickly enough that he is in such close quarters that the bladed medallion will no longer be as useful and effective.

Another attacker swings his fist widely, aiming at Daiki's face. Daiki drops his body below the swing and then delivers a series of quick punches above and below his attacker's belt. As the hood drops to the ground, the young Japanese's hand stretches forward, grabs the brute's shirt, and yanks the attacker forward and upward, throwing him into three attackers who have crept behind him. As they fall, Daiki executes a semi-circle spin, first kicking and then punching those who are almost upon him.

Daiki's foot connects with one man's face, reeling him backward into another. Still two others manage to grab Daiki from behind. The young man, using the two as support, leans backward on them and kicks upward, taking out two attackers who are nearest to him.

Arched in the air, held by the gang members, Daiki forces his feet downward. When they slam to the ground, his body weight carries the two behind him over his shoulders. As they sail overhead and feet first, Daiki stretches skyward, grabs their shirts, and yanks them toward the ground. Both thugs slam to the pavement, knocking off the wind from their lungs.

Daiki turns instinctively toward the others, but cannot escape a solid blow from one mugger who knocks him across one of the fallen men onto the concrete.

The young Japanese rolls over the man and flips immediately onto his feet. Others at his back continue to force him into the street. Five more gangsters have joined their friends, so that now Daiki has nowhere else to go. He is surrounded.

Standing in the middle of the street in front of Daiki is another gang member aiming a handgun at him. The click of a Saturday night special signals there is another weapon at his back. He intuitively steps to the side, but the sharp point of a switchblade slices into his arm.

Before the knife can strike again, however, Daiki shifts closer to the middle of the street, but now he sees the gangsters separate themselves to totally encircle him. One has a gun aimed directly at him from one position while the other aims at him from the opposite angle.

Both guns fire, almost in unison.

Daiki drops to the pavement.

MASTER SASAKI'S DOJO

REFLECTIONS
Chapter Four

D AIKI CRASHES TO THE PAVEMENT immediately upon seeing the gunmen's fingers tighten on their weapon's trigger.

Twin slugs rip through the air but with unintended results. Both bullets miss Daiki when the first one strikes the knife-wielding gang member standing behind him, sending the thug careening backwards. The second shell slashes through the shoulder of an assailant who faces the young Japanese.

In the distance, approaching headlights signal the arrival of a third party that drives a 2005 Ford Flex utility vehicle, its headlights revealing the ensuing fight. Three assailants encircle Daiki while the other gang members turn their attention in the direction of the arriving vehicle.

One hoodlum swings his blade at Daiki who ducks beneath the knife-edge and onto one hand. Balancing on one hand, Daiki kicks outward with one leg that smashes against his attacker's knee, dropping him promptly to the concrete. Using his other hand, Daiki spins rapidly in a semi-circle, sweeping the legs from under a second assailant. As his foe topples down, Daiki pushes upward with his arm while flipping his legs underneath him. The combined movement brings Daiki to his feet and faces the one opponent at his left.

IN THE DISTANCE, APPROACHING HEADLIGHTS SIGNAL THE ARRIVAL OF A THIRD PARTY.

The aggressor's stance changes when he sees Daiki's hand clutching the deadly yo-yo.

The other gang members turn toward the approaching car whose headlights illuminate even more brightly the scene of the melee. One gangster yanks a fallen brick from a dilapidated building and heaves it at the vehicle. The brick smashes against the windshield, not breaking but cracking it. Immediately, the vehicle skids to a stop; the driver's door pops open and there emerges a man carrying a heavy baseball bat.

With the purpose of overpowering the man with the baseball bat, one hood rushes forward only to discover his headlong path interrupted by the heavy swing of a Louisville slugger.

Facing the car, the three thugs converge on the shadows of the man standing behind the bright headlamps.

Daiki's arm spins his yo-yo medallion behind him to unwind it. As the speeding sphere gathers momentum and is about to approach the end of its metal cord, Daiki snaps the wheeled object in the reverse direction toward his lone attacker. The metallic disk picks up an even greater velocity as it whirls toward the knife-wielding enemy. The man has raised his knife to strike, but on the upward sweep of his arm is struck by the yo-yo that cracks his elbow and causes the knife to drop on the street.

This particular assailant has had enough. He grasps his bleeding arm and runs, frantically disappearing down a darkened alleyway.

Losing no time, Daiki heads for the car whose arrival diverted so many of the attackers. As he draws close, he hears a loud thud and sees an attacker fly out of the shadows and over the headlights, striking the ground with such ferocity that he remains motionless.

A man wielding a baseball bat follows through the shadows and light, stepping forward to swing his bat at an assailant who, having apparently been struck once, wheels backward to avoid a second blow. He goes no farther as he encounters Daiki's outstretched foot that takes him down. Before he can get up, a heavy blow of the baseball bat slings against the thug's jaw breaking its bones and rendering him unconscious.

The other gang members, wishing to avoid more deadly confrontation, flee along various escape routes that lead away from the dimly lit street. The man with the baseball bat stoops and flips over the unconscious man lying before him. He then grabs the man's wallet from the back pocket, opens it, and removes its contents of a series of fives, tens, and twenties.

"I have insurance, full coverage," says the man holding the bat, "but this should cover my deductibles."

He smiles and with one hand crams the money into his pant's pocket.

"You handled yourself extremely well. I saw that while I was pulling up."

Daiki grins and says, "You didn't do so badly with that bat either. You play baseball?"

The man replies with smiles, "Yeah. Batted 310 average my senior year."

The young Japanese rewinds his weapon and places it into his pocket when the man asks, "I saw you use that earlier. I thought it was a yo-yo."

The young man laughs and quips, "It is."

"Quite extraordinary that yo-yo of yours!" exclaims the man as he extends his hand. "I'm Ben Thompson."

"Professor Ben Thompson!" exclaims Daiki in disbelief and with a note of surprise in his voice.

"The same. And, what's your name, young man?" asks Prof. Thompson.

"Daiki," responds Daiki, "Daiki Ike."

"Ike?" repeats Prof. Thompson.

"Yes, sir," says Daiki. "It's pronounced 'e-key', not 'I-key'."

"I got it. But, listen."

"Huh?" asks Daiki.

"I mean listen," the professor insists. Both stay quiet.

Far away, they hear a rumble of trashcans and running feet gradually drawing nearer.

"We might not be so lucky this next time," says Prof. Thompson turning toward his car. "Come on, get in. Let's get out of here."

"I've got a bike, Prof. Thompson," says Daiki.

"This is a utility vehicle, it'll fit," adds Prof. Thompson as he quickly opens the trunk. "Put it in here, the backseats are down. It'll fit like I said."

Daiki lifts his bike and puts it into the wagon's trunk while Prof. Thompson closes the lid just as hurriedly. Both step to the car's doors and get in. Shortly thereafter, the vehicle pulls away just when the other gangbangers appear on the street toting clubs and knives. The only thing left for them to carry, however, are the bodies of their comrades lying on the street.

The wagon speeds away and disappears down the darkened streets.

THE FORD FLEX UTILITY vehicle, having left the tawdrier part of downtown, rolls through L.A. toward brighter streets.

"I saw you take those guys down pretty good back there, as I was pulling up."

"Thank you," says Daiki, "but, if you hadn't shown up when you did, I wouldn't be sitting here now. There were too many of them. You saved me."

Prof. Thompson smiles broadly and quips,

"Glad we could help." However, noticing that Daiki does not get the humor of "we" in his remark, Prof. Thompson continues, "My bat and I. No, that's not right, it's my bat and I and you and your yo-yo."

Daiki laughs. "Well, I'm just glad you were there when you were, Doctor."

"Think nothing of it. I have to ask: what is that yo-yo? I've never seen anything like it much less seen one used that way."

"Actually, Dr. Thompson, it's not a real yo-yo; it's some kind of medallion or jewelry or something. It's been in my family for a long time. I'm not even sure how I ended up with it. One day I got it into my mind to add a piece of string to the two-sided medallion . . . and here you go."

"I see," chuckled the older man, "a real personalized yo-yo."

"Well," says Daiki, "I've yo-yoed since I was a kid. It gives me something to fiddle with."

"I see," says Prof. Thompson.

"You teach Asian studies, Professor" asks Daiki.

"I do; more specifically, I teach Japanese religion at UCLA, but only for this semester."

"A visiting professor, right?"

Dr. Thompson nods.

"Some of my friends take your classes."

The professor glances across the seat in a perplexed manner.

"Jun Lee," rejoins Daiki.

"From Korea?" Prof. Thompson guesses.

"From South Korea," corrects Daiki.

"Oh, yes, I know her. She is in the class with

Violet Carr and Jose Rodriguez. You know them?"

"All of them," replies Daiki. I know Jun the best, but Violet and Jose are friends, too."

"They're having a lot of trouble right now, aren't they," asks the professor.

"Why, yes, Dr. Thompson!"

"The two seem to be struggling," replies the professor. "Oh, I don't mean in class; they are actually very good students."

"I know what you mean, Dr. Thompson" answers Daiki, his countenance changing with his darkening thought.

"Financially?" Prof. Thompson asks.

"Violet's dad was a big real estate broker here in LA before the bust," Daiki says.

"Oh, yes, I heard that. He went bankrupt after the Lehman Bros. debacle."

Daiki doesn't reply.

Prof. Thompson glances over at the young Japanese. He could tell that the girl's financial condition troubles him.

"I signed off on some serious student loans for each of them. I hope that helps them a little."

"It will," responds Daiki.

"From what I've heard, her family lost everything," says Prof. Thompson. Their Malibu home, savings, everything. Are she and Jose a twosome?"

The young man nods his head, but says nothing more.

"I heard about Violet's dad attempting suicide," says Prof. Thompson

"I don't think she would have made it without

Jose," adds Daiki, opening up a bit.

"They seem close," says the professor.

"More than close. Jose saved her because he understood her."

"I understand that Jose's parents were illegal immigrants; his dad was a migrant worker and his mom cleaned houses."

Sensing that Dr. Thompson already knows the story, Daiki continues, "Still they made it. Jose worked hard, got his citizenship, applied for and got into UCLA when he was 24. So yes, sir, times are still hard for them. They care for each other, support each other; they'll make it."

"I think so, too, Mr. Ike. How about you? What do you do?"

"I'm also a UCLA student."

"Majoring in Martial Arts?" Prof. Thompson jokes with a broad smile.

Returning the smile, Daiki says, "No, sir, computer science."

"Impressive. With your attitude, I'm sure you're doing well."

The Ford pulls close to a curb near a rather large rundown warehouse-like brick building. It's in an LA section that is better than the one they left, but not by much. A large metal sign hangs over the entrance, its paint flaking but still readable:

**Shotokan-ryu Karate & Kobudo Dojo
(Japanese Traditional Weapons)
Martial Arts**

"Here we are. You sure this is where you want off?"

"Yes, sir. It's where I work out and train. There's a good gym inside.

"You're going to be okay, here?" asks Prof. Thompson.

「松濤館流空手・古武道道場」
Shotokan-Ryu Karate and Kobudo
(Japanese Traditional Weapons)
Martial Arts

Mr. Eric Sasaki, Proprietor

A LARGE METAL SIGN HANGS OVER THE ENTRANCE, ITS PAINT FLAKING

"Yes, sir, I'll be fine," says Ike who opens the car door and gets out while Prof. Thompson pulls the lever that unlocks the trunk. The young Japanese takes his bike out and then wheels it to the driver's side.

"Thanks again, Dr. Thompson."

"Don't mention it. Just be careful going home, young man."

"Lesson learned. I'll be taking a much different route home."

"See you later then, Mr. Ike."

"Hope to see you, too, Doctor!" politely replies Daiki.

DESPITE THE DELAPIDATED AND tattered look of the building's façade, the interior of the Dojo is well cared for by its users. It is a large and open rectangular room with a smaller training room located on one side. Reed mats cover the lower portion of the walls, the upper half planked with dark wooden panels.

Covered with a translucent rice paper, the windows at the top of the building surround the gymnasium. Several very old light fixtures hang from the ceilings, casting a yellowish light that merges with the evening's bluish hues seeping in from the skylights.

At one end of the long rectangular room, a group of students conducts a *Souji*, or ritual cleaning, before their training session. Unlike modern-day training facilities, the Dojo is more in keeping with the Japanese tradition in that the students support and help maintain the facility instead of the instructional staff.

At the opposite end of the gym just off the main Dojo, a group of students seats on the floor of a small room. Near the far wall, a student, wearing a traditional white Karate-Gi, practices his Katas under the tutelage of a black-jacketed instructor.

The black-uniformed instructor sweeps aside the student's frontal strike and kick, while at the same time sweeping the student's feet from under him. He then places his foot on the fallen student's chest, but instead of speaking to the student, turns toward Daiki.

"You are late!" yells Eric Sasaki from across the gym. Daiki glances across the gym floor toward the tall, thin man with black, slightly graying hair, Japanese features, and piercing blue eyes.

Sasaki's father was the son of a mercantile wholesaler in Nippori Sen-I Gai, Tokyo's fabric district, and later immigrated to America. His grandfather's wife had been an American as had been his father. Each of the wives had blue eyes and the distant genes survived to give Sasaki a striking appearance with his jet-black hair and pale blue eyes.

"You are late," repeats the gym's owner.

"I'm sorry, Master Sasaki," replies Daiki, bowing politely. "I was delayed. My bike had a flat and . . ."

Sasaki interrupts by raising his hand. He excuses himself from his training pupil and quickly crosses the gym in Daiki's direction.

"I never see you in here anymore! Have you quit your training?"

"I'm sorry. My studies take so much time that I must train at the university gym. It saves me a great deal of time, and it doesn't cost me any more since the fees are part of my tuition costs anyway."

"Oh, I see," promptly counters the very serious-looking proprietor. Come with me then." Without even waiting for a reply, Sasaki turns and walks toward a doorway near the corner of the large oblong room.

Daiki follows.

Sasaki proceeds to a small, sparsely furnished office that is substantially drabber than the exterior of the building. Even shabbier is a small wooden desk that sits near a wall. Behind the desk is a series of awards, trophies, and proclamations, indicating that at one time the facility had achieved a certain level of success.

"Please sit down," says Sasaki, taking a seat himself behind his desk, while Daiki pulls up a rickety wooden chair lying against an adjacent wall.

"Tell me. How are you doing with your studies?" asks the Sensei.

"I have been fortunate, Master Sasaki. I've placed first in all my classes."

"That is good, young kohai, your grandfather will be pleased. He will know about this when I write to him."

"Thank you, Master," says Daiki.

"And your job at the library?"

"It's also going well. As you know, it's only part-time work, but they give me twenty hours a week for which I am thankful."

Sasaki takes two stamped-tan envelopes from his desk, one already opened, the other still closed. The Sensei looks at the letter from the opened envelope and studies it for a moment.

"There is something that bothers me. Your grandfather says that you have not answered his letters."

Daiki remains silent.

"You know how some people will add postscripts to their correspondence?"

Daiki nods his head, an acknowledgment that he does.

"Well, your grandfather always adds one to his. It reads like this one: 'The deeper the thought, the deeper the confusion.' What do you think he means by that?"

"I don't know," replies Daiki as he takes the letter being handed to him.

"Perhaps you can figure it out," says Sasaki.

The Sensei says nothing more and an awkward moment of tranquility passes between them. Sasaki breaks the silence.

"You do know that your grandfather is only trying to protect you, don't you? He firmly believes that your life will be in serious danger if you live in Japan."

Daiki considers his teacher's statement for a moment before commenting.

"I understand that, but I am afraid that what is not understood is how difficult my life has been under so many imposed restrictions. There is a great deal of intrigue and mystery I don't even know why I am living here. Alone! Away from my family."

Sasaki's penetrating blue eyes pierce Daiki's soul to the point where he is almost sorry he said anything in his defense. The Japanese Sensei leans forward and hands him the unopened envelope.

"He sent you this money which will help supplement your part-time work. Use it wisely and be grateful for what you have."

Daiki accepts the envelope, bowing slightly.

"All right young man. It is time for your training."

THE LIGHT FROM THE gymnasium windows appear dimmer in the evening air. Mr. Sasaki and Daiki emerge from the shadows of the now- darkened gymnasium. The young man waits while the elderly Sensei closes and then padlocks the door. Although spry for his years, it is obvious that the day has worn on him.

"Can I help?" asks Daiki.

"I am okay," replies Sasaki. "I feel as good as I did when I was twenty."

Daiki smiles.

"As long as I don't do what I did when I was twenty."

The young man's smile broadens as his instructor hands him the keys to the locker room.

"Your grandfather asked that I be your guardian while you are here. I sometimes think that I have let you down."

"You haven't," responds Daiki. "You have been a second father to me and Mrs. Sasaki ..."

"It is really unfortunate that we've lost her," sighs Sasaki deeply before adding, "I must check the other doors and windows before lockup, Daiki-san. Please remember our talk and try to make the most of what you have. One can waste a life looking at the past, seeing what is always behind, but missing what is coming."

"I understand, Master Sasaki," Daiki agrees, bowing politely. "Thank you again. I will shut off the locker room lights when I'm through."

"Please do and just turn the bolt when you leave. I will padlock it later. Good night!"

Both bow in the traditional Japanese manner, after which Sasaki steps away. Daiki walks about twenty feet and is about to enter the door leading to the locker room when he pauses before a small table leaning against the wall. On the table is a small rack that holds several Shinken or sharp practice swords. He lifts one of the weapons from the rack, and while holding it up high sees his own reflection in one of the smoky-gym mirrors that lines the wall.

Daiki's countenance as he sees himself in the mirror becomes darker. He stares at his reflected self rather with strange intensity. He suddenly lifts the Shinken high in the air and swiftly brings the sword downward and quickly spins in a semi-circle to face an imaginary opponent. In true Iaido form, Daiki executes several rapid thrusts and parries. The swift movement of the sword cutting through the air creates a strange billowy echo in the large hall.

On an upward swing, the lights turn off and darkness envelops the gym. Daiki's Iaido practice continues until he ends it with a blocking movement and counter-lunge that surely can devastate an opponent.

The rapidity of Daiki's movements, combined with his swift athletic agility, is startling and graceful yet frightful in its ferocity. It is almost as though he has transformed himself into someone else.

Daiki stops as abruptly as he has begun. For a moment, he remains frozen, fixed in place; and watched only by the strange shadows in the darkened hall whose solitary luminosity is seen through the muted light that flickers through the upper windows.

THE RAPIDITY OF DAIKI'S MOVEMENTS, COMBINED WITH HIS SWIFT ATHLETIC AGILITY, IS STARTLING AND GRACEFUL, YET FRIGHTFUL IN ITS FEROCITY.

The young man's expression remains unchanged until he moves closer to the mirror. Now standing inches away from his own reflection, tears form in his eyes.

He doesn't react or move. His face shows no sadness, yet the tears well up and accumulate. Staring at himself in the mirror, he feels a single teardrop falling from his eye and dropping in his hand that clutches the sword. The remaining lights in the building begin to extinguish and only the soft glow from a locker room stays on. No other sounds resonate in the building except for the quiet hush of a soft whisper – or a sob.

UNDER THE SHADOWS OF TAMAMO-JO

OUT OF THE PAST
Chapter Five

THE INTERMINGLED SOUNDS OF a distant Japanese countryside unite to form nature's symphony of life in a small town near Takamatsu-City, in the Kagawa-Prefecture on the island of Shikoku, Japan. The village itself falls under the shadows of the Tamamo-jo Castle, one of the most ancient remains of Japan's early culture.

A young eight-year-old boy stares through a mirror. His face, both reflective and briefly serious, he seems lost in reverie; that is, until he hears a voice calling his name.

"Daiki!"

"Yes, Grandfather," the boy quickly answers.

"Now," says an older man in his early 50s. They are in a multi-purpose structure, in a meeting hall for monks and novices alike. It is also where martial arts instructions are held as it is presently being utilized. The windows of the facility are open; and in the background is a beautiful temple that sits majestically on a nearby mountainside.

The boy and his grandfather are both dressed in a white Karate-Gi and black Hakama and are carrying the wooden practice swords called the *Bokutos*. The grandfather remains motionless while young Daiki slowly lifts his Bokuto high in the air, swiftly brings the sword downward, and then quickly spins in a semi-circle to face an imaginary opponent. He continues to execute the Iaido movement until he ends it with a blocking movement and counter-lunge.

The boy stops frozen where he is, his eyes seeking his grandfather's approval.

Not wishing to show his pride, the grandfather suppresses an approving smile while correcting the boy's final stance.

"Not bad, but it can be improved," he says.

The grandfather coaxes Daiki to face a class of twenty students, all of them about the same age, and have watched the demonstration.

"You must have observed that Daiki's movements were direct and well coordinated; but watch this," says the Grandfather, placing his hand across the boy's stomach. "He did not center and lost power as a consequence. Balance and power go hand in hand. If you lose one, you lose both," the grandfather says emphatically.

In a booming, much firmer voice, the grandfather intones, "Do you all understand?"

The students chant, "Yes, Sensei" in unison. Daiki, on the other hand, responds louder than the rest, "Yes, Grandfather."

All eyes turn to Daiki who, realizing he has addressed his teacher inappropriately, quickly shouts in an even louder voice, "Yes, Sensei."

The grandfather cannot contain his smiles.

"All right then," he adds, "let us repeat our exercise."

DAIKI AND HIS GRANDFATHER stroll down a narrow winding road that leads to the village below.

In the background, the sun's reflective light fades from the Temple as its illumination melts into that of a full moon. The sky darkens when large passing clouds partially block the moonlight.

On either side of the country motorway are rich dense forests with deep shades of green. Huge cryptomeria trees merge with tall pines and thick maples forming almost impenetrable foliage. While the moon's shafts of light throw deep shadows across the roadway and forest, the poorly illuminated images within the woodland eerily present dark, seemingly mysterious objects. To others, the evening may indicate a foreboding image; but to Daiki and his grandfather who have walked the path together many times over, this is but another night.

The roar of the nearby rushing waters from mountain-rivers and waterfalls mixes with the chirping of the night fowl and indeterminable sounds of the forest together form a cacophony of sounds. The surrounding seems to encourage deep thinking since little conversation passes between Daiki and his grandfather, until Daiki mutters impulsively, "I thought that father would pick me up from practice."

"He is a little delayed. I feel this will give us more time to spend together."

The boy smiles. "That is nice, Grandfather, yes. And so is the walk." Then changing his train of thought as young boys are wont to do, he asks, "Grandfather, do you think I will become a Jushoku?"

"Jushoku?" repeats the grandfather. "A head-priest?"

"Yes, Grandfather!"

"Is that what you want to be?"

"Ummm, I don't know, really," answers the boy. "I'm just thinking about it."

"You will have plenty of time to make up your mind, young man."

Daiki continues to saunter along, kicking a small pebble down the road. A few steps later, he catches up with the pebble and then kicks it again.

"I'm wondering also, Grandfather. Why is Father so unhappy these days?"

The question troubles the grandfather who doesn't respond but continues walking while the boy finds his pebble and kicks it again, this time off the road.

"What happened to Grandmother?" Daiki asks.

"She passed away a long time ago, before you were born."

The boy's head drops as he stares at the ground.

"You remember, we have spoken of this often," says the grandfather.

"Is that why Father is sad? He must be missing her a great deal."

The grandfather, hiding his thoughts, says nothing. From the far distance, he begins to hear the faint sounds of beating drums like tom-toms or the Taiko. Almost immediately, the drumbeats blend with the roar of a rapidly approaching automobile. Then in the distance, a dark-gray 1998 Nissan-Sentry appears.

"It's Father!" says Daiki excitedly.

"Stand still," orders the grandfather. "Do not move!"

Traveling at an ever-increasing speed, the four-door sedan swerves off the road and then back on again as it draws closer.

The grandfather hears another speeding sound. He turns to his left and faces a clump of nearby underbrush and trees. Peering through the darkness, he finds the combination of faint moonlight and shadows hard to penetrate and see anything. Then all of a sudden one of the shadows moves, forcing him to watch even more closely and intently.

The screeching tires and deafening blasts from a horn pull the grandfather's focus back on the road as the oncoming vehicle lurches on and veers onto the floor of the forest.

Daiki stiffens as he unblinkingly watches the horrific event unfolding before his very eyes. "Father . . . Father," he cries. "Mother!"

Meanwhile, the boy's father desperately tries to control the Nissan at the same time his mother involuntarily grips the dashboard.

A rustle of leaves and shadows momentarily distract the grandfather who notices an ominous figure moving away from a set of trees and disappearing behind another. The grandfather, however, forces to keep his eye on the swerving vehicle as it makes a violent turn and veers up uncontrollably toward where the grandfather and Daiki are concealed. The haunting rhythms of the tom-toms quicken and getting louder. The grandfather quickly shoves Daiki from the road; and instinctively leaps upward and over the car as the Nissan roars underneath him on its way toward a large cryptomeria tree.

Daiki hears the crash and quickly gets up only to see the vehicle engulfed by a huge fireball. Silhouetted against the fire, young Daiki staggers to the edge of the road, raises his fist to the heavens and screams his lungs out! But the roaring explosion drowns Daiki's anguished cry.

THE EXPLOSION DROWNS DAIKI'S ANGUISHED CRY.

SWEAT STREAMS FROM DAIKI'S brow as he stares into the gymnasium mirror, his eyes welling up with painful tears of distant memories, now rolling down his face. He maintains his sword position, and finally breathes deeply as he lowers the weapon. His reflection in the glass grows smaller as he walks away through the gym's doorway . . . and disappears.

WESTWOOD VILLAGE

THE FLOW OF WATER
Chapter Six

WESTWOOD VILLAGE, THOUGH A part of Los Angeles proper, is a college town, dotted with small shops that are closed on weekends when students and numerous tourists pour through them--playing, talking, laughing, and shopping, of course. Small coffee shops have always been a part of this academic setting and hardly any street fails to support at least one such establishment.

Next to a video rental and bookstore is Fontana's, a quaint coffee shop with a small outdoor-sitting area that sports a few tables and chairs. Students linger and sit there with their computers, while others rest against the shop's brick wall, vigorously exercising their thumbs as they busily read, send, and receive text messages.

Six students hurriedly pull several tables and chairs together to make an exclusive area for their larger group, and then take their seats, laugh, and sip their coffee. It's Jun, Steve, Michael, William, Jose, and Violet.

Michael takes a sip, makes a face, and says, "Arggg. Too strong! Gotta add milk to this and some chocolate flakes to the foam." As he stands to leave, Steve leans over to Jun.

"So tell me, Jun, how about tonight? I have the tickets to the late-night concert after your party!"

The conversation at the stable gets interrupted when Daiki wheels his bike nearby, dismounts while it is still moving slowly, and parks it in a bike rack. He begins talking to the two at the table even before he dismounts, "You guys finished classes already?"

"Yeah, and guess what," says Jun. "We've all made some very weighty decisions."

"To quit school?" quips Daiki.

"YEAH AND GUESS WHAT?" ASKS JUN.

"No, silly, not quitting. Come on, take a guess."

"We're going to Japan," says William walking back from adding condiments to his coffee.

"We won the lottery!" exclaims Michael.

"You've got to be kidding," says Daiki. "What lottery?" He waits for a different response, but gets none. "You're serious!"

"Absolutely," laughs Michael, his affable smile broadening even further. "The professor wants us to join him on the famous '88 Temples Pilgrimage".

"In the mountains? You're talking about Kukai's hardship journey?"

"The same," says William proudly. "But that's not all."

"What's not all?" asks Daiki. "You're talking about Dr. Thompson?"

"Yes," says Jun. The same, and we're all going."

"We?" Daiki says.

"You, too, buddy," adds William. "You're included."

"You must be kidding! I don't even take the course."

"Not kidding at all!" answers Michael.

"Wait a minute," says Daiki emphatically. "Not so fast." He leans closer to Jun so that only she can hear. "You know that Jose and Violet don't have the money for this. They can barely make ends meet."

Jun smiles a knowing smile.

"For that matter, neither do I," adds Daiki.

"Me either," chimes in Michael, "but no problem."

Jun's smile broadens, "Don't worry about it. It's all taken care of."

Now Daiki thinks that this may be the time to worry. "How taken care of? "I don't understand any of this; I don't see how you guys in particular got to be the six selected."

"Easy," replies Jun. Dr. Thompson's class has some 135 students. There are thirty-eight table desks in the lecture hall, each seating four students, with a few seats left over."

"Yeah, and our group sits together at two of them," interrupted Michael, laughing. "Talk about luck!"

"What Michael tries to say is that the professor has a research foundation that's funding the trip, but it has money only for seven people needed for the trip: six students and Dr. Thompson's research assistant who's a computer whiz."

"That's right!" exclaims Michael. "It worked out great; there were six of us at the table, with one empty seat. The research assistant made it seven."

"The fund or grant, or whatever you call it, pays all our expenses over and back," explains William."

"That's not all," interrupts Jose, "but we each get a little spending money as well. We can sure use it."

"Wait a minute. You still haven't told me how you guys were picked," presses Daiki.

"Dr. Thompson dropped thirty-four green ping-pong balls into a small box, then added two red balls. That's for thirty-six tables, get it?" adds Michael.

"He picked a student at each table to reach in and pull out a ball. Our two tables pulled out the red ones," continues Jun.

"Violet pulled the red ones out for us," said William smiling, "We were lucky, she was the one Thompson selected to make the draw."

"Which made you, my friend, the seventh man," says Michael.

"And why is that, and just how did my being the seventh-man all come about?" Daiki demands.

"Dr. Thompson asked those who won the draw to stay after class to get more information," says Steve. "And we stayed."

"While we were in the meeting," Jun tries to explain, "Dr. Thompson received a note informing him that Millie . . ."

"Who's Millie?" catches Daiki.

"Dr. Thompson's research assistant who sent a note telling the professor she can't make the trip."

"So then, Jun let another class member get the chance to go on the trip by suggesting you," says Steve, with a note of bitterness in his voice.

"I didn't ruin someone else's chance to join the trip," continues Jun, giving Steve a scornful look. "I simply told Dr. Thompson about you, Daiki. I said you were a genius on the computer and another Einstein. He needs someone good on the computer and can speak Japanese, and Millie doesn't speak Japanese. Dr. Thompson agrees with me. He wants you, Daiki, to go with us. He says you are the perfect replacement."

Jun pauses for a moment, takes a half-step toward Daiki, and looking him squarely in the eyes, quips, "And, so do I."

Steve's smile vanishes with Jun's statement even as his other friends laugh.

"You only live once, buddy," remarks William. "This is a big deal, so how about it? Are you going with us?"

The information has been almost too much for Daiki who is trying to process it all. He has other questions to ask, but the only one he can muster is, "When are all these happening?"

Jun grins, "Next month, right after school is out. So, back to the big question: you are coming with us, right?" asks Jun.

"I will consider it," says Daiki thoughtfully.

"Consider it!" exclaims Steve. "Don't insult Jun after she went out on a limb, and figures he probably already has an alternate agenda. He turns directly to Jun instead and speaks only to her.

"I will think about it. Seriously. I will!"

"Okay, then," says Jun, "Good. See you at the party tonight."

"Party?"

"Party! You do remember the promise, don't you, the one at my sorority? You are coming, right?"

After a rather pregnant pause, it is clear that Daiki not only has not planned to come but also has already forgotten the event.

"You swore," reminds Jun matter-of-factly with a tinge of anger in her voice.

"I didn't swear," retorts the young Japanese defensively.

Seeing an opening to make Daiki look bad, Steve quickly reacts, "Well, if he's too busy, we'll just have to manage without him."

No one pays attention to Steve's asinine statement, which leaves him standing alone and feeling somewhat foolish.

Daiki gives them all a passive look and really wants to refuse, but when he feels Jun's eyes searching deep into his own, he breaks into a reluctant smile and says, "Okay, you win. I'll be there for sure."

"I'll see you then. You may come with us, if you like," invites Jun.

"No, I have to go back and get some work done if I'm going to the party later. I just came down to get a cup of java to carry me through the day."

"You didn't have to do that," smiles Jun.

A puzzled look crosses over Daiki's face.

"I already got you a cup," says Jun while she points to a small table nearby where she has laid her books. Next to them are her cup of cappuccino and another cup of coffee.

"Double espresso. Straight, no cream, and no milk for you . . . right?" Jun says sweetly.

Daiki's smile broadens. "Right!"

DAIKI PUSHES HIS BIKE into a makeshift bicycle rack in the boarding-house garage. Snatching the satchel from its basket, he walks to a screen door, pulls it open, and then enters the backdoor to the house.

The young Japanese is in a good mood climbing the inside steps, taking two at a time, toward his second-floor apartment. Reaching the hallway, he passes two other doors on the way to his. An old-fashioned hall-table sits against a wall covered with antiquated wallpaper, and adjacent to a dimly lit lamp is a large vase. The dull light in the hallway and the dated furnishings cast an overall-dark-and-depressing ambience.

Daiki unlocks and opens the door to his apartment. The room is small and has sparse furniture in it. Aside from a simple work-desk, there is a single bed placed against one wall, and a small camper refrigerator against the adjacent one. Two black-and-white photographs hang above his desk. Under it are two mid-sized, high-resolution monitors connected to a top-of-the-line Apple Tower computer.

Daiki brushes the research papers and books stacked along the desk to one side. He lays his satchel near his chair, opens and empties it of its books and papers. He is about to sit down but remembers the bulge in his pocket. Smiling, he removes his yo-yo medallion and studies its strange Yin-Yang markings before placing it on his desk.

He adjusts his computer keyboard for a convenient reach and starts to turn on the computer. As an afterthought, though, he retrieves his yo-yo, lifts it again, and looks at the curious syllabic engravings on its face. Daiki turns it over and notices that the opposite side has similar engravings, but upon studying them more closely, he is able to see the innate difference. He recognizes the Hiragana, Katakana, and Kanji style; but they seem mixed in a very limited way with some Latin scripting.

Making no sense of the markings, Daiki places the yo-yo aside and turns on his computer. Waiting for the computer to boot, he looks at the pictures above his desk. To his right is a photo of his grandfather, and to the left is an attractive Japanese couple dressed in traditional wedding attire.

Daiki gazes at his grandfather' photograph, and suddenly loses himself in thought.

ON ONE OF THE DOJO'S REED MATS, grandfather sits opposite Daiki. Before them are three bowls of water: two contain clear water and one holds a murky liquid. In front of each set of bowls is a larger bowl nearly twice the size of the two others and filled with clear water. Grandfather lifts the first of the three water bowls.

"Look into the bowl, young man. Tell me what you see."

"Dirty water, Grandfather."

"Can you drink it?"

"I would not want to, Grandfather."

"Is the water fit for bathing?"

"Not either, Grandfather; it is not."

Daichi pulls the larger bowl containing the clear water toward his grandson. "Would you drink of this?" he asks.

"Yes, Grandfather."

"And could you use it for bathing?"

"Yes, Grandfather, of course."

Daichi holds the murky bowl over the larger one and slowly empties its contents.

"You can see that the dirty water changes the color of the clear water," says the grandfather.

"Yes, Grandfather," replies Daiki, "and it does so very slowly."

The grandfather nods, continues to empty the contents, and then sets the smaller empty bowl beside the larger bowl of contaminated water.

"Do you see what is wrong here, grandson?" asks Daichi.

"The larger bowl of clear water is now also dirty. We cannot drink it or wash with it," answers Daiki.

Daichi smiles and says, "That is correct, young one. The small bowl of dirty water standing over time does nothing but gather impurities. The larger bowl, however, fills itself from a steady flow of water. As the water flows, it rids itself of filth."

"The small bowl is not part of the flow of water and does nothing to protect itself. Do you understand it, grandson?"

Daiki starts to shake his head to show that he does, but then says, "No, Grandfather!"

"The dirty bowl is like one's integrity that has become dark," explains the grandfather. "It is one made filthy by the wrong elements added to it until the water is useless and fouls all that it comes in contact with."

The grandfather pours the dirty water back into the smaller emptied bowl; it spills over and there yet remains tainted water in the larger bowl.

"When honor is lost," continues the grandfather, "whatever remains ruins what is around it. When water flows, the water stays clear; it keeps its integrity and honor. However, when it allows the dark water to mix with it, it loses its purity, its integrity, and its honor. So it is with all people."

The grandfather pauses cautiously then adds, "Remember, young grandson, all evil begins with a single dark thought or dishonorable act. If allowed, it will expand and overtake you and then proceed to overtake also those around you."

The grandfather pours the residual dirty water from the large bowl into the remaining two small bowls. Soon all the water becomes dingy.

THE FLOW OF WATER

"Honor and integrity of the mind are more important to the proper flow of water than all the training to prepare the physical body," grandfather says.

"How do I keep the dirty water away from me?" asks the young boy.

"Do nothing to muddy it," answers the grandfather. "Keep your word, remain loyal to those who have helped you; flee from the reach of evil, but if it comes upon you never fear to fight it."

The boy processes what his grandfather is saying to him, then reaches for his bowl of dirty water and pours it on the ground. He lifts the larger bowl of clear water and fills the smaller one. Now, the once-contaminated bowl overflows with clear water; Daiki replaces the bowls, and sees that no dirty water remains. He raises his head toward his grandfather who moves his gaze from his grandson's bowls, then looks and smiles at Daiki.

"You have learned of honor in and through the flow of water."

DAIKI IS AWARE HIS COMPUTER HAS BOOTED. He turns on the computer monitor that displays various symbols for different computer programs. He selects one called *Satellite* and immediately enters some keystroke commands. An image of Japan soon emerges. He presses the program's zoom feature and the screen image enlarges to an enhanced close-up of this nation of islands. He clicks the zoom feature once again and the images pushes closer until only Shikoku Island appears. Daiki clicks another key and the screen transitions to the island's Soto Temple. He studies the temple briefly and then enters keystroke commands that produce a series of newspaper headlines. The first one reads:

> **Car Crash Ruled Accidental**
> *No foul play involved, rules coroner.*

Daiki glances up from his computer when he hears faint sounds of strange-beating drums. Unable to detect their source, he decides that they are coming from the outside and have nothing to do with him. He goes back to his computer.

Delving deeper into the online newspaper files, he reads another account of his parents' deaths.

> **Strange Death of Temple Priest Unexplained.**

Then another . . . this one accompanied by a picture of his grandfather at a much younger age.

> **Temple Priest Daichi Ike Distraught**
>
> *Soto Temple Priest Daichi Ike's assertions that his son and wife were victims of a murderous plot have been attributed to a father's grief at the tragic demise of his only son. The Ikes were found burnt to death inside the . . .*

The strange drumbeats magnify and perhaps getting closer. Daiki walks to the window and peers out into the deepening late-afternoon shadows. The once-louder drumbeats cease; and seeing nothing, the young man returns to his desk.

Strangely, the monitor's image has reverted to that of the temple as a third headline fades up on his second monitor.

> **Ike Family Finally Laid to Rest**
>
> *The remains of the Ike Family were finally interred at*

Daiki clicks on the video that accompanies the headline. The clip opens at the Soto Temple

Cemetery on Shikoku Island, Japan. In the background is the image of the temple that was previously on the screen. The burial ground, lined with old gravestones placed close together, sits atop a higher ground than where the temple is.

A large number of monks in the Ike funeral are in their formal black attire; all the others wear dark suits and black armbands.

The Monks' voices rise as they sing their sacred Shugendo music. The presiding priest stands at a small portable dais and raises his hands for the music to stop.

The priest recites a sutra over an urn that Daiki understands contains his family's cremated remains. Behind the priest is a tombstone that the video news camera reveals to bear the names of his mother and father.

The news-clip shifts to shots of others in attendance. Among them is the boy's grandfather whose face saddens as the urn is lowered into the grave. When the news video zooms into a close-up of the urn, it shows the priest, now in the background, removing a set of papers from the podium.

The beating drums get louder. Daiki glances up from his desk but quickly returns to his monitor and rewinds and freezes the image of the priest when . . .

Sounds of the Taiko no longer resonate from outside the apartment. Instead, they seem to be coming either from the apartment hallway or directly from outside his door. Daiki pushes back his chair, leaves the desk, and walks directly to his door.

DAIKI PUSHES BACK HIS CHAIR, LEAVES THE DESK AND WALKS DIRECTLY TO HIS DOOR.

"Come on Michael . . . if this is one of your pranks," he shouts as he flings open the door.

The drumbeats cease all of a sudden, but the hallway is empty. Daiki shakes his head, steps back inside his room, and returns to the monitors. One monitor shows a new image. He studies it for a moment. The enlarged shot of the paper held by the priest puzzles him. The cover sheet is typed and reads:

"Treasures"
By Jiro Yamada

The Unpublished Work of Kukai's Final Days

Daiki scribbles a note on a pad and then scrolls further down on the enlarged picture. At the bottom is another typed notation:

```
Archived property of 88 temples.
```

HE TRIED TO AVOID HER BY LOOKING AWAY; BUT THE
MORE HE AVOIDS HER, THE LOUDER SHE GETS.

APPARITIONS
Chapter Seven

T HE APPROACHING EVENING CASTS dark shadows across the two-story brick- and- stucco sorority house. There are commercial torches placed throughout the front lawn. Daiki rolls his bike onto the sidewalk and heads toward the area near one of the large hedges where bicycles are parked. As he pulls up, he hears someone calling his name.

"Daiki, Daiki, over here," yells a cute blonde in a white blouse and faded-denim shorts.

"Oh, no!" Daiki says to himself. "Donna Loftus." She is in his program and attends several classes with him. He knows she likes him, but finds her far too boisterous for his taste.

"Hey, Daiki! Come help me with the torches," pleads Donna.

He tries to avoid her by looking away, but the more he tries the louder she gets. Finally, in desperation, he gives up, looks in her direction, and waves at her.

"Hi, Donna! Please wait a minute; I need to park my bike and check inside. I'll be back right out."

"Don't forget me now," hollers Donna, even louder than before.

Daiki is almost certain he will just as soon forget . . . as soon as possible. He wheels his bike to the rack and slides it into one of the slots. As he steps away, he lingers to look at the house, one of about twelve on Yancey Street, and one of the avenues known for fraternity and sorority activities.

Music blares from strategically placed speakers, and the sorority house itself seems to vibrate with the percussion sounds of the pounding refrains. It is still early and others are just arriving. Five or more students are laughing, drinking, and carrying conversation outside the house, but most of the activities obviously are happening inside.

Daiki is about to ring the doorbell when the door abruptly swings open and unexpectedly startles him.

Several students exit and one of them, a girl in jeans and a dark-green, checkered-blouse, addresses him.

"No need to ring; come on in." With that, she's gone and Daiki proceeds inside. Others brush by him as he meanders through the throng of students, and he definitely feeling lost in the crowd.

"You're here," says someone poking him in the back. He turns around and it's Violet, but before he can say anything, she asks, "You want to hear a little secret?"

Left on his own, Daiki may have said no, but she gives him no chance.

"I've been pinned!" exclaims Violet who pulls out a beautiful fraternity pin with a small diamond neatly set in the center. She beams with pride, but then notices Daiki's blank expression.

"You don't know about these things, yes?" pokes Violet. "Well, over here when a man "pins" a girl, it means he wants her to be his."

"It's Jose, right?" Daiki guesses.

"No, it's Steve."

Daiki looks shocked.

Laughing hard, Violet continues, "Of course, it's Jose, silly."

She grabs Daiki by the arm and pulls him through the noisy crowd into a side room where William and Michael are talking.

"Hey buddy, over here," yells Michael waving Daiki over.

Daiki waves back and walks in Michael's direction. Getting near where his friends are, Jun Lee appears right in front of him. For an awkward moment, he just stands there, not sure of what to do. Jun, however, certainly knows what she needs to do. She puts her arm around his and leads him to a quieter corner of the room.

Steve, meanwhile, has been watching the two together and doesn't like what he has just witnessed. On top of it, William makes a deriding comment, "It looks like Daiki has your girl."

Without a word, Steve walks away and goes toward Jun and Daiki's direction.

Standing close, Jun asks Daiki, "Are you coming with us?"

"I would like to, but I don't think that I'll be able to."

"Do you ever think of going back?"

"To Japan?" asks Daiki.

"Yeah, Japan."

"Of course. Why do you ask?"

"You never talk about it. You're always so . . . so mysterious."

"May I have this dance?" interrupts Steve.

"Oh, I'm sorry, Daiki just asked me," replies Jun, half dragging Daiki across the floor to an area where students are dancing."

Steve is left alone on the floor, standing by himself. He is most unhappy.

The music is a slow one, and as Jun and Daiki dance across the floor, she pulls closer to him and at one point lays her head on his shoulder.

Not too far from the dancing partners is Steve who has moved to a dark corner of the room. His anger simmers as he glowers at the two Asians dancing together, one song after another.

IT'S WAY PAST MIDNIGHT now. Outside the sorority house, most of the students are leaving the party. Daiki says a quiet goodbye to Jun and waves at the others before heading toward the bike rack. To his surprise, his bike is nowhere in sight. Gone!

"It's over here," calls out a familiar voice.

Daiki recognizes Steve Chan standing in the shadows of the larger hedges. Peering further, he sees his bike lying on the ground.

"I hear you're some kind of a big-shot Japanese Martial Artist," says Steve, sarcastically.

"I know some."

"Yeah, well, I'm Chinese and I've studied Shaolin Kung Fu, the oldest traditional Martial Arts in existence!"

"Yes, in China," agrees Daiki emotionless and with a straight face."

"And I've studied *Jeet-Kune-Do*," adds Steve.

"Have you? I've always liked the Bruce Lee films," responds Daiki, again without feeling.

None of the conversation is sitting well with Steve who obviously believes himself to be the superior Martial Artist. He says, "I always heard that a skilled Kung-Fu expert can teach a Karate guy any day."

"Maybe," replies Daiki walking toward his bike. "I wouldn't know."

"Oh? Well, then, I think it's time you and I tested the theory," arrogantly insists Steve. "It's time that I taught you a thing or two."

Daiki reaches down to lift his bike and sees that the lock remains intact. But when he starts to lift the bike, Steve steps on the tire rim forcing the bike to the ground.

"Move your foot, please!" requests Daiki politely.

Steve remains in place, clenching his fists at his side.

"I said move!" Daiki says with urgency. This time, however, the young Japanese is neither polite in tone nor in manner.

Steve, standing a foot taller that Daiki, shifts his balance to his right leg as he adopts the traditional Shaolin Horse stance with his legs spread wide, left fist out- stretched, right arm arched upward, and fist clenched even tighter. He stares hard into Daiki's eyes, a direct challenge no doubt from Steve.

Daiki heaves a sigh, then moves away from his bike which is still lying on the ground, and settles into a more natural position opposite Steve. Daiki's stance is more relaxed with his legs spread shoulder-length wide and his hands open and fingers spread, not clenched. With his arms spread outward, Daiki stares directly into Steve's eyes. The two adversaries watch each other closely as one begins to circle the other.

Steve is clearly far taller, heavier, and stronger than the lither Daiki, an observation that is not lost on Steve's opponent.

YOUNG DAIKI SLAMS AGAINST a tree as a larger, stronger opponent attacks and strikes him repeatedly. Daiki tries to fight back but is overpowered by the sheer size and strength of his Steve's. A powerful kick to the stomach sends Daiki breathlessly to his knees. Steve shoves him backward, and snatches Daiki's leather-and-cloth satchel, and then turns to run away.

But the bully runs directly into Daichi Ike who has been standing unflinchingly when Steve bounces off him. Before the bewildered thug can stand up, Daichi already has taken back the stolen satchel from Steve's grasp. The older man's icy stare chills the Steve who loses no time fleeing from the scene.

Daichi helps his grandson to his feet. My counter offense was as useless as my defense."

"How did you see all that?" demands the grandfather.

"His size. His strength," stammers Daiki.

"You were already defeated even before you began."

"I don't understand it, Grandfather," pleads Daiki defensively.

"You must have Kyoujin, a strong mind and spirit," replies the grandfather. "He who thinks he is losing before he has begun has already lost."

STEVE CHAN MOVES CLOSER and circles Daiki who's waiting for a frontal assault. But before that can happen, Steve rushes forward, attacking Daiki from the side, then backs away. Daiki is able to block the first strike but misses the second one, which smashes hard to the side of his face. Before Daiki can recover, Steve rushes again toward him from another angle, this time striking hard with short quick punches at the body.

Daiki reels from the punches and feels the impact of Steve Chan's larger size and weight. For a moment, doubt creeps into Daiki's mind. Trained in the traditional Japanese Martial Arts that relies heavily upon frontal straight-line attacks, he is not used to this multiple hands-and-short-range combat. In response to the rapid onslaught, Daiki backs away from Steve who now has gained confidence and becomes even more aggressive, striking his opponent with successive blows and kicks.

Daiki is surprised by Steve's speed and Kung Fu techniques, which he has never encountered nor experienced before. As he staggers from the assault, Daiki suddenly remembers his grandfather's words: *"He who thinks he is losing before he has begun has already lost. You must have Kyoujin!"*

The young Japanese braces with resolve, looks for an opening and carefully studies Steve's movements.

DAICHI AND HIS GRANDSON train alone in the gym. Young Daiki appears to be doing well when the grandfather changes his approach, throwing the grandson off guard, thus obtaining a quick advantage over him. Daiki seems lost; and sensing his grandson's sudden confusion Daichi stops and addresses him.

"Listen to me . . . very carefully."

The confused young boy stops--stands with his head bowed--and listens.

"One drop of falling water is of no value. But many drops gathered together can make a storm that fills a tiny stream. The stream may become a larger river and then an ocean, even a powerful tsunami."

The young boy raises his head and tries to listen hard and understand what his grandfather is telling him.

"But the tiny drops of water," continues Daichi, "to become a powerful tsunami must flow uninterrupted toward its goal. It must avoid rocks, branches, or any other obstacle to its flow. Then, once it gathers together, it can destroy, swallow, and flood its objective."

For a moment, Daiki stares directly into his grandfather's eyes, then nods his head in full and silent comprehension.

"You see, Daiki, the same is true in fighting. It is not the size or power of your opponent. It is how you have gather yourself together like the flow of water."

"But, Grandfather, what if my opponent has gathered a great flow of water himself?"

Daichi smiles, "Then you must decrease and diminish your opponent's flow so that his power weakens while yours strengthens."

STEVE RUSHES TOWARD HIS smaller foe once more, swinging and kicking in the air; Daiki backs away, successfully blocking his Steve's blows, thus reducing his power. Steve delivers a powerful blow but Daiki darts to one side, misses him and causes the blow to overshoot its target, throwing Steve off-balance.

Steve immediately spins to deliver another blow, but once more Daiki is not there. Steve topples slightly and then feels a mild shove on the side accompanied with several rapid blows that sends him down to one knee.

The fall is all but unexpected and though Steve is surprised, he recovers quickly and changes his stance to the *Tai Zu Chang Quen* or the Emperor's long-hands technique. He has noticed that Daiki appears calmer and, unlike Steve, is no longer circling but remains stationary, though continually facing his adversary.

Without warning, Steve moves rapidly forward and then twists into a position to deliver a high kick to Daiki's body. To his surprise, he sees Daiki rushing full speed directly at him.

Steve brings his knee close to his chest, and as Daiki gets closer, extends his foot viciously in his foe's direction. Like before, Daiki is no longer there. Instead, he springs upward, somersaulting high over Steve, rights himself in midair and let fly with a hard kick that connects at the back of Steve's head.

Having lost his balance, Steve staggers forward from his unconnected kick. Daiki's somersault blow, however, does connect and Steve finds himself flying across three bikes before landing face down. The hard thud knocks the wind out of him so that all he can do is lay there.

He rolls over to see Daiki staring down at him.

In Daiki's mind, he hears the echoing words of his grandfather, *"If your opponent is larger and stronger, you must avoid direct hits because his power and size will overcome you. Fight wisely and remember that your size will not matter if you master the philosophy of the flow of water."*

Daiki stands in a commanding posture. Steve tries to get up but is too winded; he loses his balance and falls backwards again. Unable to do anything, he tries to close his eyes when he hears his rival speak, "Here!"

Opening his eyes, Steve sees Daiki offering his hand as a help-up. He takes it and while standing, says, "You know, I love her."

"I know, Steve. But Jun is a big girl. She can make up her own mind."

Steve says nothing as Daiki lifts his bike, unlocks it, and then rides away.

Three other students claim their bikes and leave. The party is over and most everybody is gone. Through one of the windows, Steve watches Jun help others put away the decorations.

Once more, Steve is standing alone; alone to ponder Daiki's parting remark. Perhaps it's that comment that hurts Steve the most..

THE UNIVERSITY OF CALIFORNIA is a huge one with sundry rooms and sections that serve its many academic programs. Daiki has visited all of them but prefers the one he is in now. It's a large room with long-wooden study tables, most of which are piled high with books and papers while students prepare their term papers toward the end of the school year. Behind the tables on either side of the room are library shelves that contain hundreds of volumes it takes to support the university's curriculum. This particular room has traditional wooden shelves along the wall with stacks of metal shelving at each end. Several lamps and soft overhead lights illuminate the room, but none too brightly. Overall, the library has a soft, warm, academic and scholarly feel to it.

To Daiki's right, two professors stand together, each discussing the publications that they are currently engaged in writing. The young man didn't mind the low hum of conversation. In fact, he enjoyed the "intellectual buzz" that fills the library. That, coupled with the feel one gets when surrounded by books, created an ideal study environment for him.

His computer blinks as another application pops up. Daiki was finishing his part of a group work project that was due Monday for the *Multiprocessor Synchronization* course he was taking. He studied the diagram in front of him, applying first one analytical tool and then another. If one were describing Daiki, they would say he was focused. Perhaps that focus made him fail to notice that he was being observed. In fact, he had been closely watched for the past ten minutes.

"Good Morning, Mr. Ike," says the observer.

Not expecting to be called by name in this library's inner sanctum, the recognition startled the boy. Then, he recognized the speaker.

"Oh, I'm sorry, I didn't see you there, Dr. Thompson."

Daiki started to rise but was interrupted by the professor, "Don't bother to get up. I won't be long."

"Can I help you, sir," requested Daiki.

"Mr. Ike . . . do you mind if I call you Daiki?

"Sure, I mean, no not at all. Of course."

"Well, you know I'm going to Japan at the end of the school session."

"That's all that my friends talk about. It seems their table won the draw."

"Yes, they did. Did they tell you that I have a research foundation that's paying the way for six of them plus a research assistant?"

GOOD MORNING, MR. IKE. DON'T BOTHER TO GET UP.

"Yes, sir. Jun told me."

"As it turns out, I have a much greater workload than I'd planned on. Not that I mind because they're sponsoring my research assistant who's handy on the computer. I'm not."

"Great," replied Daiki.

"Not so great. She can't go. In fact, she had to drop out of school yesterday and is already gone. Some kind of trouble back home, I understand."

"I'm sorry to hear that."

"That's why I'm here. Your buddy, William Strong, was over in the student center and when I asked about you, he told me that he thought you'd be here."

"What can I do for you?"

"I need you to replace my assistant on the trip. It can't be just anybody, but someone with a solid understanding of computers, the Japanese language and culture of the place where we're going."

"I appreciate the offer, Dr. Thompson, but..."

"It will be worth your while of course," interrupted Thompson. "Your hotel, travel and food expenses are paid for. Furthermore, there is a very good fee in it for you. I'm guessing that like most college students, you could use the money?"

"Of course and, your offer is very generous but I must decline. I promised my Grandfather that I'd do nothing until my studies are finished. I'm close to the end now but I must take summer classes so I can finish next year."

For a moment, Dr. Thompson says nothing but then he shakes his head and starts to walk away. "I'm the one who's sorry, but I do understand. I have to travel up to San Jose for a few days so I can't fill the position right away. If you change your mind, please call me. Here's my number," he said, handing Daiki a business card.

"Thank you again, Professor. If anything changes, I will."

"You're a good student, I looked up your grades. And, you are very focused. I watched you work for a few minutes and nothing interrupted you. You speak Japanese and lived on the very Japanese Island that we're visiting. I earnestly hope that you change your mind."

Then, the professor smiled, "I know that Jun Lee hopes that you do as well."

Daiki blushed, but didn't reply.

"Good day, Mr. Ike."

"Good day, Dr. Thompson," replied Daiki.

The professor ambles away, disappearing behind the metal stacks at the end of the room.

DAIKI SWINGS HIS ROOM door open as his hand automatically moves to the light switch. As the room brightens, he tosses his satchel onto the bed, lays his cellphone on his desk, and quickly crosses to the small refrigerator, opens its door, removes a Ginger Ale and loosens its detachable cap.

Returning to his desk, he pushes a keyboard button, which is immediately accompanied by the familiar sound of a computer booting up. He sits, quickly enters some commands, and watches as both computer screens display a series of newspaper articles and headlines. All of them deal with the Ike Family tragedy.

Suddenly, the boy pauses. He strains to hear some sounds that he thinks he hears but hearing nothing, returns to his video and with a few more commands, is once again watching his family's funeral. When the newscast reaches the priest with the papers, he enlarges the image until he once again reads:

"Treasures"
By Jiro Yamada
The Unpublished Work of Kukai's Final Days

The young Japanese quickly scrolls down the image until he recognizes the line:

[Archived property of 88 temples.]

Daiki shifts his attention to the first monitor as he makes an entry on his computer: *"Treasures" by Jiro Yamada.*

Web pages display immediately, but nothing related to the referenced book, only listings of Jiro Yamada websites.

The boy Googles a second reference: *Unpublished works of Kukai's last days*, but finds nothing. He's puzzled, so he enters the final words from the paper, *"Archived property of 88 temples."* No response either. Instead, a list of temples appears on the screen. Disgusted, he reenters, *"Treasures" by Jiro Yamada.*

Suddenly, Daiki's attention is diverted. He cocks his head slightly as if that will help him ear the sound he is searching for. Then, he hears it; the faint beat of tom-toms, the Taiko.

The boy pushes back from his desk and walks to the window, opens it, and leans out. He can hear the drums but is unable to tell where the sound is coming from.

Daiki shakes his head as though giving up then pulls back inside and this time closes both the window and the blinds, apparently hoping to lessen the sound. It stops.

The young man returns to his desk and is surprised to see a new pop-up on his screen.

However, he's unable to read it because it shifts back and forth on the screen, making the words illegible.

"Aggggg," cries Daiki, both angry and frustrated. He moves his pointer to the top of the page and clicks *refresh*. Immediately, the sounds of the drums begin again. Only this time they have multiplied in number.

And – the incessant beating is drawing closer. The cellphone on Daiki's desk rings but he ignores it.

Abruptly, the computer speakers begin to transmit the identical haunting sounds of the Taiko leaving Daiki surrounded by the drumbeats. He hits the keys on his keyboard in an attempt to switch off the computer, but to no avail. Finally, he reaches for the plug and yanks it from the wall but the image not only remains on the first computer screen but then crosses over to the second one.

The Taiko tom-toms beat louder as the image of a large cavern encompasses both monitors. The indistinct popup abruptly clarifies, reading:

"BOOK NO LONGER AVAILABLE"

The popup vanishes only to be replaced by a monk wearing a black lacquered cup strapped to his forehead. A second monk wearing a similar cup materializes in the screen's foreground. An indistinct mantra starts and grows louder, *"namah samanta vajraaNaaM* ------- even as the foreground image, glowing a shimmering white, begins to detach itself from the monitors and hover in front of both screens.

Daiki tries to focus his mind on the sights, sounds, and spoken Japanese but as he does so, the computer screens take on an eerie green glow even as the remaining monk inside the left monitor radiates with a contrasting white iridescence.

THE FOREGROUND IMAGE DETACHES FROM THE MONITORS AND HOVERS IN FRONT OF BOTH SCREENS.

The chant, *"namah samanta vajraaNaaM, caNDamahaarosana sphoTaya-------"*, very deep-throated and bass-like, increases to mask the angry Japanese being spoken by both figures to each other. Daiki ties to understand but the more he strains to hear the more light-headed he becomes.

Without warning the room shakes as though from an earthquake. Daiki struggles to stand in order to escape but cannot. The room spins as the boy falls to the floor. He screams but no sounds are forthcoming, and just as he loses consciousness, the sound of the beating tom-toms overtake all others.

And then, Daiki hears nothing!

THE LAX BRADLEY INTERNATIONAL-TERMINAL HUMS WITH ENDLESS ACTIVITY.

THE TRIP
Chapter Eight

THE CELL PHONE ON THE DESK rings, stops, and then rings again. The ringing jars Daiki who shakes his head and hopes it may help lift him from his trance-like stupor.

The ringing stops then starts again, its sound echoing strangely in the small room. His mind getting clearer, Daiki raises the receiver and tries to answer it with an instant, "Hello!"

Nothing is heard from the other end, nothing but dead silence. It's obvious there is a caller, but whoever or whatever it is, the telephone stays silent.

"Hello," repeats Daiki. The silence changes to a boring hum; the caller has hung up.

Daiki studies the one image left on his computer: the temple. And then he smiles.

THE LAX BRADLEY INTERNATIONAL-TERMINAL at Los Angeles, hums with endless activity. At the check-in counter of Trans-Nippon Airway, a group of students busily sort through their luggage before boarding. Jun and Violet talk excitedly while Jose, Steve, William, and Michael handle the boxes and suitcases. While Michael's parents joke with Jose's grandmother, Violet's father wonders whether the young students may get lost going to and returning from Japan.

"Hey," shouts a voice in the distance. It is Daiki who races toward them. "Sorry, I'm late; horrible traffic!"

Jun rushes gladly toward Daiki, grabs and hugs him to his sheer embarrassment. Steve's countenance darkens as he watches the two walk toward her luggage.

Michael lets out his infectious chuckle as he helps load his friends' luggage at the checkout counter. Without losing a beat and like an announcer, he shouts at the top of his voice, drowning the terminal noise over, "You're just in time to help, Daiki. This is one way to build muscle for our journey," he says.

"I'd rather do it another way," Steve says in dismay, stealing a glance at Daiki who begins to help Jun with her luggage.

Dr. Thompson hands a series of passports to another airline attendant who looks them over before handing them back to him.

"Keep these with you. You'll need to show them again as you board."

"Yes, ma'am," replies Dr. Thompson who leaves the counter and walks toward where the students are and proceeds to return their passports while passing along the attendant's instructions.

"Okay, everyone, all pieces of your baggage have been loaded and you have each your passports," says Dr. Thompson. "There's a coffee shop upstairs where you can say goodbye to your family," and then glancing at Daiki's direction adds, ". . . and your friends."

Everyone leaves for the coffee shop except Daiki and Jun.

"I'd rather say goodbye here," says Daiki.

"It's a shame that you're not going," asserts Jun rather matter-of-factly.

"I wouldn't call it a 'shame'," quips Daiki.

"You know what I mean, silly."

"I do, just kidding. I would like to go, but certain things don't allow me to. I just can't."

"I still don't understand what you're saying, but what I do understand is that you just can't leave and not say goodbye to your friends," says Jun.

"I know but . . ."

"And to Dr. Thompson who saved your butt."

Daiki sighs as Jun takes him by the hand and pulls him up the escalator toward the coffee shop.

Violet's father waves at his daughter as he starts down the escalator, accompanied by Jose's grandmother who is also waving. As Violet watches them leave, she draws closer to Jose. Laying her head on his shoulder, she says sweetly, "Jose, this will be the best trip, ever!"

Jose smiles, pulls her closer and lays his head on hers.

Steve walks behind them and asks, "Excuse me you two, but I need to ask Violet something.

Inside the *La Coffee' Mediterranean* shop, Jun, Daiki, William, and Michael pull some chairs around several tables, surrounded by pieces of carry-on luggage, for everyone to sit together.

Violet and Jose walk in, along with Steve who waves his ticket.

"Hey, Jun, good news . . . we're sitting together. Violet has changed seats with me, yes, indeed," says Steve as he turns to face Daiki and arrogantly mutters, "It seems that fate has taken over."

"JOSE, THIS WILL BE THE BEST TRIP, EVER."

"Some fate," quips Michael. "Looks like a disaster to me."

Others laugh but Steve does not.

"Listen, everybody," calls Prof. Thompson as he enters the coffee shop. "If you need or want anything from duty-free, better get it now. We don't have that much time."

Jun stands up, takes Daiki's hand, and pulls him behind her and says, "I'll meet you guys at the gate."

Steve's countenance morphs into an angry frown when Jun walks away with Daiki. Prof. Thompson yells after them, "Hey, guys, wait a minute."

The two stop and turn around as the professor approaches.

"Listen, Mr. Ike . . . Daiki. If you change your mind, let me know. I can make passage arrangements from over there."

"Thank you, Dr. Thompson. It's very tempting. It really is, but I have personal obligations."

"I understand, but should you change your mind, you know how to reach me," Prof. Thompson says almost pleadingly and then continues his way to the coffee shop. After a few steps, however, he stops and turns back toward Jun and Daiki and knowingly, happily adds, "Besides, from where I stand, you can make some girl very happy."

Thompson heads back toward the coffee shop, while Jun remains stationary.

"He's right, you know," she says. "I'm going to miss you."

Daiki blushes, something not lost on Jun.

"I worry about you. This is an opportunity for you to return home, see your family, but you don't take it. Are you planning on staying in the U.S. forever? I mean, are you going to make your career here?" Before Daiki can answer, they hear a familiar voice.

"Come on Jun, we're late," shouts Steve, now standing with her carry-ons in front of the coffee shop. "They're waiting for us."

"I have to go," says Jun. "They won't let you come with me any farther."

Daiki nods; he fully understands.

For a moment, Jun gazes into Daiki's eyes and then turns to go. She takes a few steps, but stops and walks back to him.

"I have something for you," she says while removing her sorority pin and quickly fastens it onto Daiki's shirt.

"There, you keep it. Keep it close . . . close to your heart."

Before Daiki can answer, Jun has stepped away and joins the others walking toward the gate. He watches her walk down the corridor and disappear around the corner.

Briefly, the young Japanese stands quietly and sighs and turns to leave when he sees Jun poke her head around the corner. She smiles sweetly at him and then vanishes once more.

THE HUGE TRANS-NIPPON airliner finally soars up above the city. Inside the plane, passengers adjust themselves for the first leg of their long journey. Some airline hosts take drink orders while the other passengers wait for the signal that allows them to operate their electronic devices.

From the ground, Daiki looks up the sky where the plane has been and now long gone and out of sight. He remembers another flight he had taken long ago; one he took when he was a very young boy.

A SMALL FEEDER LINE JET is parked on the tarmac of a local Japanese airport. A few yards distance from the jet, a chain link fence separates a group of passengers and the plane. Young Daiki is one of the waiting passengers. His grandfather, Daichi Ike, checks his grandson's jacket and carry-on luggage, all in a vague attempt to conceal the pain he feels because of the boy's impending departure.

"You have your passport? Money? Ticket from Tokyo to Los Angeles?"

The young boy nods mechanically to his grandfather's inquiries.

"Now, remember the names of the people who will meet you when you arrive in Los Angeles."

"I will, Grandfather."

"The Sasakis will look after you. You have their photograph; don't lose it.

"I won't, Grandfather."

"Good. Now be . . ."

"How long will I have to be away?" interrupts the little boy with tears welling up in his eyes.

"I don't know," says Daichi turning his head away to avoid showing his emotion, "I will send for you as soon as it is safe."

A flight attendant approaches them, bowing slightly as the grandfather rises.

"Mr. Ike, Flight 38 to Narita is ready for boarding."

The grandfather bends down and gives Daiki a long, tight hug. The little boy wants to cry, but fights back the tears as the attendant takes his hand and leads him away into the plane. When they reach the gate, the boy turns his head for one last glimpse of his grandfather.

Daichi waves goodbye and then shouts, "Daiki, do you have the . . .?" pointing to his neck.

The young boy lifts the chain around his neck and pulls up a medallion from beneath his shirt. It's shaped like a yo-yo hand with an engraved Yin-Yang symbol on each side.

"I have it, Grandfather," Daiki yells back.

Smiling, Daichi Ike shouts again, "Do not forget, I will be with you–even if I am not there."

The young boy smiles sadly and then follows the attendant through the boarding gate.

"YOU'VE GOT TO LOVE this view," Dr. Thompson exclaims, pointing to the scenic mountain while Jun snaps an IPhone picture.

"You know, guys," says Michael. "I've never thought about Japan having mountains."

"Aside from Mt. Fuji?" quips Steve.

"Well, yeah, duh?" Michael replies. "I know about Mt. Fuji."

Everyone in the car laughs.

"Fujiyama is located on another island, Honshu," clarifies Dr. Thompson. "It is Japan's highest mountain, standing about 12,388 feet high."

"It's a former volcano, isn't it, Professor?" asks Violet.

"There's nothing former about it," replies Dr. Thompson. "It's still active, although the last eruption was back in the 1700s."

"Forget about that," jokes Michael. "I don't want to be under it if it goes off again."

"I see," interrupts Michael who changes the subject. "Is it me or is anyone else having trouble with everyone driving on the wrong side of the road?" he inquires. "Seems backward to me!"

Prof. Thompson and Jun laugh.

"The driver's side is on the right," says Dr. Thompson. "Just like in England and other countries. Maybe, we're the ones driving on the wrong side."

Dr. Thompson guides his small rental Toyota wagon along a winding road. While he continues to point out scenery after scenery, the others remain busy taking pictures and sending text messages.

"We'll be at the hotel soon," says Dr. Thompson.

"That's too bad," says Jun. "This is so beautiful. I wish we could drive around some more."

"Me, too," exclaims Michael. "You don't get to see this stuff every day."

Steve frowns, "Not me, I'm exhausted. This has been a long trip."

"It'll be midday when we get to where we're going," says Dr. Thompson. "If any of you want to, we can take a drive after we check in and freshen up."

Michael is the first to say yes, followed by Jun. Steve and William mumble something under their breath, while Violet and Jose are too engrossed in their own conversation to say much of anything to anyone.

"Say, Dr. Thompson, what's our hotel like? Where are we staying?" asks William.

"Oh, it's a very fancy one. Plush! You'll like it," replies Dr. Thompson.

The vehicle speeds down the ever-narrowing roadway toward its destination.

ACCOMPANIED BY THE PROFESSOR, the young students struggle as they climb upward along a rugged dirt pathway. With extra gear strapped to their backs, they all carry their own luggage.

"Fancy, he says!" moans Michael who is huffing and puffing while readjusting the load on his back and in his arms.

"No kidding," immediately agrees William who's shifting a particularly heavy suitcase to his other hand.

Jose, carrying his load and part of Violet's, is red in the face from the uphill exertion. He pauses on the trail in order to catch his breath.

"So, what's this place really like, the one that we're going to, Dr. Thompson? Are we actually going through all the austere training, fasting, and the like that you were talking about?"

"Absolutely, along with spiritual purification and chastisement."

"Oh great! That's reassuring, indeed," interjects Steve who is also putting his bags down.

"And sitting under freezing ice-cold waterfalls. Yes, really, that will be real training," remarks Michael.

"Violet's not going to like this," says Jose.

"Hey, buddy, I'm just teasing you," responds Michael. "There are lots of things she can do here. I'm told that some people come here to find love."

Jose sighs; Steve smiles at Jun who simply looks away.

Dr. Thompson stops by the groaning group and announces, "Okay, young people, let's keep going, we'll be there shortly."

"Great, I can't wait," mumbles William under his breath.

"What's that, William?" asks Dr. Thompson.

"Can't keep up the gait," replies William, trying to cover up his previous remark.

DAIKI'S CELL PHONE BEEPS signaling an incoming text message. He clicks his phone and there's another snapshot from Jun. He smiles and reviews the continual flow of pictures from her trip. Thus far, she's sent him photos of the master weavers of Yukata who use cotton dyed with natural indigo. There are also numerous scenic images of mountains, trees, and waterfalls.

As Daiki views the new picture of the group climbing a steep path, his hand passes over the pin that Jun gave him. He knows that it's a big deal for a sorority member to give someone their pin, because even though it belongs to the sorority member, the pin must be returned to the organization when the member dies. Daiki, for his part, is unsure what to make of this and he is uncertain how he should react to Jun's gift.

A second message accompanied by another photo appears. The picture is one of a large bell standing in front of an ornate temple set high in the mountains. It is truly breathtakingly beautiful!

THE PICTURE IS ONE OF A LARGE BELL STANDING IN FRONT OF AN ORNATE TEMPLE SET HIGH IN THE MOUNTAINS.

Another beep is heard, indicating an incoming new text message. This one, too, is from Jun and reads:

This is where we're staying on Seto Island in the Sea of Japan. LOL. Hard climbing but beautiful. Dr. Thompson said he would take us sightseeing but so far, Michael and I are the only ones up to it. Wish you were here!

THE TEMPLE BELL

CRASH
Chapter Nine

J UN REPLACES HER PHONE in a handbag as the group draws closer to the temple. She passes the highly decorated bell that she has just photographed, and notices that it is even larger and more ancient than she thought.

Two monks, robed in green and yellow, stand under the blue-tiled Japanese roof housing the solid brass gong. Each grasp one of the two ropes attached to a huge pole suspended before the bell and began to swing the column. The mallet end of the pole strikes the brass producing an unexpected deep-throated boom that echoes repeatedly throughout the mountain countryside.

As the temple bell reverberates, a second-in-command priest, the Fuku-Kancho, recognizes Dr. Thompson and approaches with both palms raised in a greeting, "Professor Thompson. Welcome to Tenkai-ji Temple. We are delighted to receive you and your American students."

Thompson returns the priest's bow as the students, weary from their trek, drop their gear onto the ground.

"This is where we're staying?" questions William in a hushed whisper to Steve.

"Yeah, I think so."

"What happened to the fancy hotel Dr. Thompson was talking about?" asks William.

The Fuku-Kancho smiles as he addresses the students, "We welcome all of you to our one-thousand-year old fancy hotel."

William blushes at having been overheard, but Thompson, amused at the students' bewilderment, replies, "It was a very kind and unexpected invitation and such a generous offer. We thank you."

"It was our Kancho who issued the invitation."

"That's the head priest," whispers Michael to William. "This guy is second in command."

"Please, come with me," says the Fuku-Kancho, "Our monks will help you with your bags."

The students are led up a series of steps to the temple's entrance.

"Please enter," says the Priest, "Lunch will be served shortly but first let me show you around."

The Fuku-Kancho leads the party inside where rays of colored lights stream from tall narrow windows casting irregular shadows on the temples' fitted teak plank-wood floors.

On one side of this mysterious temple, a series of red wooden bars set in front of the tiled wall on which a figure of a dragon resides. At the very end of the temple stands a large shrine dominated by a huge statue of a man. On each side, stand figures of hideous demon servants.

"This is En no Ozunu," says the Fuku-Kancho.

Violet clutches Jose's hand even tighter. "Those things are frightening," she murmurs.

"They're just statues but very realistically done. Nothing to worry about," says Jose reassuringly.

AT THE VERY END OF THE TEMPLE STANDS A LARGE SHRINE DOMINATED BY A HUGE STATUE OF A MAN.

"You will remember our class lessons," says Thompson, addressing his students. "En no Ozunu, is the founder of Shugendo."

"That is correct Dr. Thompson," interjects the Fuku-Kancho. "The great En no Ozunu taught us many noted principles and we will endeavor to pass some of them along to you while you are here. It is important to prepare your mind as you develop your bodies through our rigorous training."

"Rigorous training!" exclaims William quietly.

"Of course, what did you expect?" replies Michael. "Don't be a 'wuss'!"

William looks askance at Michael and is about to reply, when the Fuku-Kancho interjects, "You will need both mind and body to complete the pilgrimage that you have traveled to Shikoku Island to achieve."

William, still complaining, mumbles, "Something tells me I'm gonna hate this."

The Fuku-Kancho turns and stares unsmilingly, directly at William. There is a moment of awkward silence and then the priest says, "When you complete your training and the pilgrimage, you will be a changed person – a better human being."

The students follow the priest as he exits the temple but William, lagging behind, whispers ever so quietly to Michael, "What is this? He's got ears like Superman."

Michael shakes his head, "You are such a 'wuss'."

The students leave the Temple, exiting into the deepening afternoon shadows.

DAIKI, ENJOYING THE EARLY morning, passes the Sasaki Gym sign, opens the door, and steps into the dojo. Mr. Sasaki waves to him from across the floor. The boy waves and proceeds to the locker room where he grabs a "karate-gi" from his locker and begins to dress for a workout.

The sound of Daiki's cell phone ringing is amplified in the hollowness of the locker room. As he lifts it from his shirt pocket, a text message appears. A look of surprise crosses his face. The message is from Professor Thompson.

It reads:

> Hi Daiki, too bad you aren't with us. Everyone is having a wonderful time, especially Jun. Check your e-mail. I've just sent you an old document. Take a look at it when you have a chance. All the best, Ben.

Daiki is puzzled at the message's reference but as he click's the phone's email application, he sees the same message, only this one has the attachment.

DR. THOMPSON DRIVES ALONG the country roads in the late afternoon sightseeing trip that he had promised his students. As Jun had earlier predicted, only she and Michael were up to taking the long walk back to the car so they are the only ones taking the trip.

"Thanks for showing us around some more," says Jun, riding in the back seat.

"You're welcome," replies Thompson. "Besides this gives me an opportunity to go back to the village and pick up some supplies that we'll be needing later."

Michael sitting in front, leans backward toward Jun, "I don't think Steve was too happy about being left behind."

"That's an understatement," says Jun.

"Had to be done," says Thompson, interrupting. "I needed them to start cleaning our facilities.

"Yeah, Steve loved doing that . . . sweeping the floors and cleaning out the Japanese toilets," laughs Michael.

Professor Thompson and Jun join the laughter.

"Well, it needed to be done and its part of the training. Besides, I'll need help carting the supplies back to the temple when we get back. That won't be all that easy. We'll get settled in and then tomorrow, we can begin our research. We'll probably divide into groups with one researching the Kin-ji Temple facility."

"The one near to Tenkai-ji?" interrupts Jun.

"Yeah," replies Thompson. "William speaks Japanese so I'll let him take Steve, Violet and Jose. The travel is best suited for the four of them. The area's fairly safe but since Steve can handle himself; I'll assign him to that group as well. The rest of you will remain with me at Tenkai-ji."

"By the way, Jun, thanks for letting me sit up front," says Michael. "This is my first time to Asia and I want to get as many good photographs as I can."

Thompson explains the various scenic vistas of Seto Island as they tour while Michael remains busy snapping pictures. The sun turns a golden brown as it settles behind the clouds on the low horizon, reflecting a purple sky that highlights the landscape.

"Let's stop here for a moment," says Thompson as he pulls the car to a curb where local vendors are selling food and drinks among other wares. "We'll reach the village below us in another half hour or so but I'm thirsty. Let's grab a drink."

The professor exits the car followed by his two students and speaking in Japanese, orders a drink for himself and the others.

"They're made from a special fruit-blend on

the island. You'll like it."

"Thanks, Professor," says Jun.

"We're all set, now," replies Thompson. "Let's get back in, and continue on."

The threesomes drive for another twenty-five minutes, when Jun spots twinkling lights in a valley just below them.

"Isn't that where we're going?"

"So it is Jun, so it is," replies Thompson.

Michael snaps a picture when suddenly a bright light flashes across his face.

"It's another car," cries Jun. "He's traveling fast and I don't think he's going to make the curve."

A car careens around the curve, rapidly bearing down on Thompson's car. The driver of the approaching vehicle panics and brakes hard in an attempt to avoid a head-on collision, but in so doing, skids on the road and smashes into a mountain barricade.

The car bounces off the barrier and swipes Thompson's car. Dr. Thompson over-steers to correct for the impact but begins to edge off the road. For a moment, it seems that he has the vehicle under control when another sharp bend comes into view. The professor pulls at the wheel but too much so. The car skids, leans slightly, and then flies over the embankment and into a gully, picking up speed as it rushes toward a large tree at the end of the gulch.

The Toyota wagon smashes into the tree and catches fire. The airbags discharge immediately and afterwards; Michael and Thompson try to escape but are wedged in by the tree and their seats.

THE CAR FLIES OVER THE EMBANKMENT AND INTO A GULLY, PICKING UP SPEED AS IT RUSHES TOWARD A LARGE TREE.

Jun lies collapsed in the back seat. She briefly opens her eyes and attempts to rise before passing into unconsciousness.

The blaze increases as it sweeps over the car and threatens to encompass the entire vehicle.

CANDLELIGHT FLICKERED MYSTERIOUSLY ACROSS THE ROUGH-HEWN WALLS OF A LARGE ANCIENT STONE PASSAGEWAY.

ENTER TENKAI-BO
Chapter Ten

DAIKI'S BOARDING HOUSE room is unlit and Daiki is sleeping when suddenly his cell phone lights up, followed by ring tones. Sleepily, the boy's hand stretches across his lone nightstand, grabs the handset and answers.

"Hello!"

"Daiki, this is William. William Strong!"

"Yes, of course. What is it? It's late."

"Something awful has happened. Jun was in an accident."

Daiki sits up in the bed, awake and concerned, "Is she okay?"

"She has a bad concussion, but the doctors think she'll be alright."

"That's a relief," sighs Daiki.

"That's not the worst of it," says William. There were two others in the accident."

"Who?"

"Michael and Professor Thompson."

Daiki says nothing but takes a deep breath as if preparing for the worst.

William continues, "They were both killed in the crash."

Daiki is stunned by William's disclosure and for a moment, feels paralyzed by the shock but slowly; a look of determination passes over him.

"I'm coming over. I'll catch the next plane out."

A LARGE TRANS-NIPPON AIRWAYS jet flies through the late evening sky, passing in front of a full moon faintly covered by approaching storm clouds.

The cabin lights are dimmed and most of the passengers are in various stages of sleep, but not Daiki. Wide-awake, he stares through the slightly curved windows into the dark night. It's cooler in the cabin so Daiki pulls his blanket closer around him but it cannot cover the guilt he's feeling. He is haunted by the fact that he refused to return to Japan when Dr. Thompson asked him to. Thompson had saved his life when the street thugs had tried to kill him. Daiki had a duty to the professor because of that. But still, he had given his word to his Grandfather that he would not return to Japan until after graduation.

Daiki sighs, his mind trying to reconcile the conflict. "Duty or Promise?" he asks himself. "My grandfather always taught that duty is first, above all. But am I returning not out of duty, but out of guilt? He reflects for a minute. "No, Grandfather would have me fulfill my duty to Dr. Thompson first. It must be duty before promise."

More than once, the Grandfather had said, "When all is gone . . . when everything is lost, our word must remain." Now, Daiki feels he has lost more than two of his friends. He has perhaps lost honor.

Daiki pulls the blanket even closer and shuts his eyes.

An attendant walks down the aisle, cautioning passengers to fasten their seat belts, "Please buckle up," she says. "The Captain has just turned on the seat belt sign. We'll be running into some turbulence ahead."

Daiki's mind returns to an earlier turbulence of his youth.

A LARGE TRANS-NIPPON AIRWAYS JET FLIES THROUGH THE LATE EVENING SKY.

DAICHI STANDS WITH HIS Grandson in front of a carved headstone that is erected in a large traditional Japanese cemetery that is located near the temple.

The Grandfather closes his prayer as he lowers his head in a moment of silence. He glances at little Daiki by his side and sighs. He turns to knell beside his grandson. As he does so, he removes a beautiful Medallion from his jacket. On both sides is the familiar symbol of the Yin-Yang.

"This was your father's. I presented it to him when he became the temple priest. I am sure that he would have wanted you to have it."

"Where did you get it, Grandfather?" asks Daiki, taking the Medallion from his grandfather.

"It was first given to me by my teacher, Kaien Priest, many years ago. I was still young, around twenty."

Daichi drops lower so that he is at eye level with his grandson. "You must guard this with your life, young Daiki."

"It is important Grandfather?"

"Yes, it is and it is very sacred. May it protect you and keep you on the enlightened path of Shugendo, for all of your days."

The grandfather stands, places his arm around the child and leads him down a dirt path toward the Temple.

"It pains me greatly, but I must tell you that you cannot stay in Japan."

"But, why?" says the boy, now very alarmed upon hearing this news.

"There are many things that I cannot tell you at this time. Later perhaps."

Confused, the boy asks, "Are you leaving with me?"

"No," replies Daichi.

"Then, why can I not stay with you?"

The grandfather pauses for a moment, then answers. "Because you must trust that I am making the right decision for you, for the both of us."

"Remember the teaching in the flow of water. If a stream is pulled in two directions, the current weakens. The path of a man is determined by his destination and his destination by the direction he takes. The force of his mind shapes that direction, which determines his destination. Like water, if you divert the flow, you weaken the path. In the "Flow of Water", your path keeps your mind strong and your "Kyoujin", your spirit undefeatable. You must trust that I am choosing the right direction for you, for the both of us."

"I understand, Grandfather!" replies the child.

The two continue on but behind them, some distance away, three men wearing civilian clothing emerge from the trees and cautiously follow them.

COULD I GET YOU something, else?" asks the airline hostess.

Daiki is lost in thought and fails to hear the question.

"Sir. Would you care for something else to drink?"

The boy glances up from the series of text messages on his Smartphone. "Oh, I'm sorry. Just lost in thought here. No thanks, I'm fine."

The hostess smiles and moves on to other

passengers.

Daiki more closely examines one of the messages. It is a muddle of strange symbols, letters, and numbers. He scrolls up and down the message trying to make sense of what appears to be some sort of riddle. Shaking his head, he scrolls to the top of the message. It reads:

From: Ben Thompson <Thompson@netcast.net>
Date: Monday, July 7, 2014 6:47 PM
To: "Daiki Ike" <daikii@gmail.com>
Subject: puzzle

Below it was the only part of the message that Daiki could understand, and he didn't comprehend that very well, either.

The deeper the thought the deeper the confusion!

"What was Dr. Thompson trying, to tell me?" asks Daiki, who was troubled by the unfathomable message he'd received on his Smartphone, on July 7th, the day Professor Thompson was killed.

Below the message were the mysterious symbols followed again by the same message.

Suddenly, Daiki remembers his grandfather's letter, the one that Mr. Sasaki had given him in the gym. Daiki rumbles through his backpack, retrieves the letter, and rereads it. In it were the same words from Dr. Thompson's text message, "The deeper the thought, the deeper the confusion."

Daiki is even more confused.

"I don't understand," mumbles Daiki under his breath. "I don't understand this at all."

DR. THOMPSON'S TEXT MESSAGE, "THE DEEPER THE THOUGHT, THE DEEPER THE CONFUSION."

CAPTAIN MASAO SATO, the police Captain of Kagawa Prefecture, Shikoku Island, sits at his desk as his assistant, Norio Himura, types notes on an old electric IBM Selectric typewriter. Steve, Violet, William and Jose are seated in front of the desk and Mr. Winston James, an America Embassy official, stands before them to the right of the desk.

143

The young people are being interviewed in a rural police station located at the foot of Shikoku Mountain, near the village's hospital.

"Please sign these statements then you are free to go," says the embassy official.

The students sign the documents as Mr. James continues, "We have notified Mr. Wood's family, but we have no address for Professor's Thompson's next of kin."

"I'm afraid that we can't help you, Mr. James," replies Steve.

"He was our professor but we didn't know anything about his personal life," adds Violet.

Captain Sato stands, handing them copies of the documents they've just signed. "My condolences to all of you. This is a terrible tragedy for us at Shikoku. We rarely have accidents like this, especially ones that are fatal. I am deeply sorry."

The police Captain shakes their hands while handing them their copies. "If I may be of any help, please let me know."

"Thank you Captain," replies Steve, the last to shake Sato's hand. Afterward, he follows his friends through the door and exits the building.

Sato walks to his office's one window and gazes at the departing young people.

"Anything wrong, Captain Sato?" asks James.

The Police official, an older man in his early sixties, doesn't reply immediately. Instead, he steadily watches the students as they leave the police station grounds, in the direction of the nearby hospital.

James, puzzled at not getting an answer, asks once again. "Is there anything wrong, Captain?"
"I wonder," replies Sato. "I wonder."

ONBOARD THE AIRLINER, Daiki has unpacked his laptop and offloaded Dr. Thompson's text message.

THE PUZZLING IMAGES, WHICH DISPLAYS THREE CIRCLES, FILLED WITH CHINESE CHARACTERS.

Daiki studies the larger images, which seemingly display three circles filled with Chinese characters. Superimposed over them is a prominent five-point star shaped figure. At the end of each tip are larger characters. However, in the center of the star is an even larger character.

Daiki studies the characters situated at each of the star's points. As he does so, he moves his computer pointer over each of the Chinese figures while murmuring their translations to himself. "Wood, Water, Metal, Fire, and Earth, the five elements of the Taoism universe? I don't understand this."

Pointing to the large character in the center, Daiki whispers, "And the sword?"

CANDLELIGHT FLICKERS MYSTERIOUSLY across the rough-hewn walls of a large ancient stone passageway. Along one wall, an elderly Shugenja monk carefully lights the candles inside the darkened corridor. The monk is poised to light yet another candle wick when the faint sounds of beating drums echoes within the primal hollow. He freezes as he detects a shadow emerge from the darkness. At first it is an indistinct shape but then it transforms into a larger flowing indistinct form, expanding in size until if fills the side of the wall facing the elderly monastic priest.

The monk turns from the shadow to face an enigmatic figure stepping from the darkness. A tall hooded monk, imposing in size, appears to glide rather than walk along the dark stone floor. The drumbeats increase in volume as he draws closer. The elderly monk, obviously fearful, recognizes the approaching specter.

Bowing very low, his head turned down, not up, speaks his name, "Tenkai-Bo!"

The ghostly figure's face remains hidden by the dark cowls of his hood as he passes through a long corridor leading to a new, more brightly lit, chamber, which opens wide and resembles the architecture of an ancient Japanese Emperor's ceremonial gallery. Its torch-lit illumination is both dark and foreboding.

Tenkai-Bo gracefully slithers toward a raised stage on which stand two Yata-ha Shugenja warriors on each side and thirty some others on both sides. A large single cushion in the center of the platform remains empty. Below the dais, the hall extends at least fifty yards outward in all directions and is filled with hundreds of monks attired in black Shugendo clothing. They sit in a cross-legged lotus position, facing the platform with their heads bowed.

Tenkai-Bo says nothing as he surveys his followers, his commanding presence hovering ominously above them. Then raising his arms outward, he speaks.

"Yata-ha Shugenja! I have brought you here for something of consequence."

The imposing figure's voice is mechanical, deep, terrifying, and powerful. He lowers his arms, moves to the empty cushion and seemingly floats to a seated position. His unseen face, shadowed by a heavy cowl, remains turned toward them.

"I bring you good news of vital significance."

The Yata-Ha chant in approval as they raise their heads in unison. Distant drumbeats increase in volume and meld with the fanatic chants. The sight is frightening as they all wear strange masks in the shape of black-colored semi-human raven faces.

Slowly, the apparition sweeps his cowl aside unleashing a massive covering of light bluish green feather-like hair, flowing above a frightening countenance. He turns his face towards his followers and as fearsome as his disciples appear, Tenkai-Bo is even more so. The phantom wears a green half-human, half-bird like mask such that the overall effect of the monks, their leader, and the eerily lit chamber presents a macabre cultish vision of incredibly disconcerting proportions.

The Shugenja on the platform seat themselves next to Tenkai-Bo, but sit lower in position. Two are seated on one side and two on the other. The remaining thirty monks stand to the rear of the platform. In contrast to their master, these monks wear white ravens' masks and white Shugendo outfits.

Again, Tenkai-Bo raises his arms, which instantly brings the chamber to an unsettling quiet.

"You were summoned here so that I could report the significant changes that are occurring. Which will impact our collective future. These changes are emerging, indeed unfolding, even as we meet."

Tenkai-Bo's voice evokes as much authority as his physical presence. It is staccato, brusque and commanding, the voice of an Emperor.

"These are the developments that I, Tenkai-Bo foretold. They represent both the beginning and end of our noble undertaking. Your training has been hard and severe. You must expect more of the same and the sacrifices that will yet be called for, are many."

The specter glances to one side and then the other, allowing his words to sink in.

"But, these sacrifices will bring you rewards beyond comprehension, fulfilling dreams beyond mortal understanding. You are to be part of a new order . . . One that will not only transform our nation state, but the world itself."

The hall erupts with exclamations of support as the sounds of surrounding Taiko tom-toms increase in volume until the combination is deafening. Yet, all in this phantom-like chamber continue to cry in unison finally transitioning to a melodious chant that itself beats in union with the phantasmal like pounding of the unseen ancient drums.

Tenkai-Bo seemingly floats upward to a standing position. His illusory form steps forward, with arms raised higher, and outstretched arms commanding even more attention as he speaks.

"Today . . . at this moment . . . we gaze into our past from which we will create a new future . . . a new future that will transform the world as the world knows it – but not as we know it."

The roars of approval become nonstop, each growing louder than the previous one.

Tenkai-Bo pumps his fists twice with a singular fury as he shouts, "You are the first chosen but you are not the last. Thousands will follow your footsteps. They will spread firestorms across the world. These storms will be of such wrath and fury as has never been known before or will ever be known again. Others will in turn follow them until we overwhelm and sweep away all who stand before us . . . all who would dare defy us . . . all who would keep us from our rightful heritage!"

The demonic figure lowers his arms, his powerful voice quieting, "A miracle is transpiring before us . . . a miracle that comes from the heavens above and from the abode below."

Those below the master shout their approval.

"And why is it that we will succeed? Why is it that no one will have the power to stop us?

The Yata-ha scream in unison, "Tenkai-Bo, Tenkai-Bo, Tenkai-Bo!"

Tenkai-Bo lifts his arms high, "Swear your allegiance!"

"Tenkai-Bo, Tenkai-Bo, Tenkai-Bo!" screams the followers. "We swear, we swear!"

"Swear it again," booms the leader's commanding voice.

The drums beat louder and more rapidly, overtaking even the wildly fanatic chants of the followers of this monastic figure standing before them.

Tenkai-Bo has entered!

TENKAI-BO HAS ENTERED!

TENKAI-JI TEMPLE

THE RETURN
Chapter Eleven

"**K**OU? WHAT DOES THIS MEAN?**"** Daiki asks himself.

"I'm sorry, what's that?" inquires the passenger sitting next to him.

"Nothing," replies Daiki, smiling. "It's nothing. I'm doing some Japanese translations on my computer and came up with something that I don't understand?"

Daiki stares at the computer characters spelling out the letters KOU.

"I see," remarks the passenger. "I thought you were speaking to me. Sorry."

"That's okay," says Daiki, "I didn't mean to disturb you."

The plane's sound system carries a woman's voice who instructs the passengers to prepare for landing.

"Ladies and gentlemen: As we start our descent, please make sure your seat backs and tray tables are in their full and upright position. Make sure your seat belt is securely fastened and all carry-on luggage is . . ."

"Looks like we're finally landing," says the passenger who begins fastening his seat belt as does Daiki.

The plane touches down on the runway at the regional airport on Shikoku Island, Japan. Daiki breaths a sigh of apprehension, he has arrived.

DAIKI PARKS HIS RENTAL car outside Shikoku Island's rural hospital and then enters through its front entryway. Stopping at the receptionist's desk, he asks directions to Jun Lee's room and finding out, quickly makes his way there. He finds her door closed, pauses for a moment, and then gently knocks before entering.

Jun sits in bed, with William, Jose, and Violet around her. Steve, meanwhile, sits on an upright chair next to Jun and is talking to her when Daiki walks in.

"Daiki! Thank God, you're here!" exclaims Jun. Steve, feeling self-conscious, stands up.

"How are you doing, Jun?" asks Daiki.

"Me? I'm fine. Bruised a bit, but much better, now!" she replies.

"The doctor says Jun might be able to leave here in a week," interrupts Steve.

Turning to the others, Daiki asks, "What about Michael . . . and Prof. Thompson?"

Jose and Violet are nervously uncomfortable as they glance at each other. Steve places his hand on top of Jun's.

"We've had a terrible time," explains William trying to explain as well as break the tension in the room. "We're half-guessing but the professor must have lost control of his car and gone over the embankment and into a tree; that's what must've done it."

"It's a miracle Jun survived at all," Steve adds, tightening his grasp on Jun's hand.

"The temple is making the funeral preparations," says William, "as well as arranging for the bodies to be shipped home."

Violet begins to cry and Jose quickly moves to hold and comfort her.

"Many things trouble me, William," says Daiki.

"Like what, Ike?" asks Steve rather brusquely.

"First of all, the accident itself," replies Daiki. "Secondly, there's this very strange message I received."

Steve stiffens as he asks, "What kind of message?"

"From Prof. Thompson," replies Daiki.

"What does it say?" inquires Jose.

"Are Dr. Thompson's belongings still in his room?" probes Daiki, ignoring Jose's question.

"Yeah, I think so," says William.

"Why do you ask?" insists Violet.

"I want to search his room. There may be something there . . . a clue perhaps."

"Good idea," says William. "Come on, I can take you there."

"Steve and I will go with you," throws in Jose and then adds, "Violet, why don't you stay with Jun?"

As the four start to leave, Jun cries out quietly, "Daiki, I'm happy that you have come back home...to Japan."

Daiki smiles as Steve glances at Jun uneasily, who continues, "I'm just sorry that it is under these circumstances."

INSIDE THE EVENING SHADOWS of a dark parked Nissan, a foreboding figure watches as William, Daiki, Steve, and Jose leave the hospital. As the four drive off, the menacing form lifts his cellphone and in a soft whisper says, "They are just leaving now."

The man pauses, listening to an unheard inquiry on the other line. He then responds, "Yes, Sir, he is with them."

THE TENKAI-JI TEMPLE sprawls across several acres of cultivated woodland. A large pagoda to one side of the tiled-roofed building, houses a huge bell that stand in front of a ten-foot circular brass gong. A body of water partially encircles the temple at its entrance and streams around other structures that are built just behind the channel. In the distance, several mountain peaks jut skyward, their western sides reflecting the setting sun.

Several dormitory complexes are constructed adjacent to the temple and Daiki parks his rental car close to the first building, and then along with his companions, leaves the vehicle and enter the residence hall.

Once inside, William leads the others down a narrow corridor that leads to the room where Prof. Thompson stayed.

"Here it is," says William, stopping before a Shoji sliding door. "It's unlocked," he utters as he slips open the rice-paper sliding screen.

Four large framed black-ink drawings adorn the ceilings from north and south to east and west.

"Strange," whispers William in a quietly solemn voice. "What to make of this?"

At the north end of the ceiling is a dramatic drawing of a turtle snake, while on the opposite end on the south is a phoenix. Displayed on the east side is a dragon, and a tiger on the west.

On the floor are a series of eight Tatami mats made of straw.

"Yep, I think I like my sleeping quarters better," says Jose in the same quiet tones as William's.

"What exactly are we looking for," inquires Steve.

"I don't know," responds Daiki. "His research papers, sketches, notes, anything. We'll bring back whatever we can find."

The four continue to search the room, busily shifting through drawers, and shelves; even the professor's luggage located in one corner of the room. William snatches a number of books from a small table set against one wall and loads them into an empty trash bag that he has removed from a nearby wastebasket.

"What's this?" examines Jose.

The others turn in Jose's direction as he withdraws a long tubular cardboard container from an open cupboard door behind the turtle-snake, which is one of four black-inked paintings hanging from the ceilings. He hands it to Daiki.

Daiki opens one end and removes a cylindrical piece of silken parchment.

"It's a scroll of some sort," says the young Japanese. "Let's open it."

Daiki carefully unrolls the scroll on one of the mats. The moonlight from the small window streams across the scroll and casts a strange pale-yellow translucent light over its surface.

"This is original," says Daiki who takes a deep breath while trying to stand up.

"What is it?" Steve asks.

"Anything wrong, Ike?" William asks urgently.

For a moment, Daiki stands motionless, saying nothing. Then he slowly turns toward the others and proclaims, "It's real!"

"What's real?" queries Steve.

"This document was created by Kukai!"

"What? How did Prof. Thompson get it?" William says incredulously.

"There's no telling, but this thing must be more than twelve hundred years old."

Daiki leans forward to study the scroll more closely.

"Wow! What a work of art," blurts Jose. "Good thing we found this."

"This is much more than a work of art," says Daiki emphatically.

"Much more than what?" asks William.

"There's a riddle concealed in the document. It's written in ancient Japanese."

"You can read it?" Steve says in a challenging tone.

"My grandfather taught me when I was a child," continues Daiki as he points to several characters in the document. "Look! There seems to be a map hidden within the inner riddle."

THIS DOCUMENT WAS CREATED BY KUKAI!

"What do you mean?" begs William.

"There's some sort of treasure."

"A treasure map! I knew it!" exclaims William. "We're rich."

Each of the four look at one another in stunned silence, a silence that is finally interrupted by Daiki.

"Guys, check out of your rooms as quickly as possible. Everyone, bring your gear to Jun's room at the hospital. I'll meet up with you later."

"Okay, I got it," says Jose as he slides open the Shoji door that leads to the hallway.

"Aaiiiiieeee!" he screams as he quickly steps backward.

Standing at the doorway is a Fuku-Kancho priest who blocks the opening. He smiles slowly.

"Did you find what you were looking for?"

"Yes, we did," replies Daiki as he puts back the scroll into its tubular container. "Thank you, Sir." Daiki places the tube under one arm, snatches William's partially filled trash bag and then leaves the others behind to explain their having to move to a new location.

DAIKI DRIVES HIS CAR along the familiar roadway of his childhood. His mind vividly recalls details and geography of this desolate countryside. The sky continues to darken, the gathering storm clouds rapidly covering a disappearing moon. As the automobile rolls along the country highway, periodic flashes of lightning illuminate the mountains and surrounding forests.

An extraordinarily loud clap of thunder is followed by a sudden burst of heavy downpour, thus making road visibility extremely difficult. Daiki eases off the pedal, slowing the car a bit; he's fully aware of the more dangerous driving conditions right in front of him. As he steps on the brake, the tires get stuck in a patch of mud and water, causing the vehicle to skid and spin. The car swirls on the wet pavement and abruptly heads toward a thicket of ditch, trees, and brush.

To regain control of the car, Daiki quickly turns his wheels into the skid and slightly increases its speed. The wheels straighten and the spinning stop, but the vehicle continues down the narrow road.

"Whew," breathes Daiki in relief. "That was close; way too close!" Then he remembers his grandfather's instructions to him when he was a young boy.

"It is natural to be afraid, but you must force your mind to be afraid later. At the time of greatest danger, you must be calm like an uninterrupted flow of water. Fear slows the mind and stalls the body. Release your fears but only after you have first reacted and the danger has already passed."

"Thank you, Grandfather!" says Daiki aloud, pleased with himself for not panicking. "You always know what you're talking about."

In the distance, his grandfather's temple sits amidst a large clump of trees. Intermittent flashes of lightning produce a strange strobe-like effect upon the temple, an effect that increases as Daiki's car draws closer.

Daiki pulls into a long gravel driveway that leads to the temple, parks his car, and hurriedly gets out. But before he can reach the temple's portico, he is drenched with rain. Eyeing the surroundings, he notices that the temple's once-prized gardens are overrun with weeds and rubbish, all of which make the sanctuary look terribly shabby and dilapidated. Even the tombstones around the temple are overgrown with undergrowth and bedraggled groundcover. The entire place appears completely deserted. After a brief pause, he knocks on the heavy wooden door. No one answers.

"Grandfather," calls Daiki. "Grandfather, it's me . . . Daiki!"

He tries to open the door but finds it securely locked. Walking to a window to the right of the entrance, Daiki peers in but sees no one inside. However, he is shocked to see that everything else inside is disordered and unkempt. It's obvious to him that no one has lived there for years. Once more, Daiki attempts to open the door, but it is tightly barred. He moves to the right side of the temple close to the living areas. He tries the oaken door, but it is also securely locked like the entrance door.

There's a long rusty screwdriver lying against a wall on the terrace, and Daiki picks it up and uses it to pry open an adjoining window. Right away, he slides through the opening and into the living quarters.

Daiki isn't surprised to find the living room desolate and in total darkness. Only deep-shadowed forms tell Daiki there is something there at all. Then he finds himself struggling to understand what has transpired, but in the process fear slowly creeps over him.

"At the time of greatest danger, you must be as calm as the uninterrupted flow of water," Daiki can still hear his grandfather's words that echo in his head.

"I'm trying, grandfather," replies Daiki to the imaginary voice. He takes a slow, deep breath and centers his focus on the fear that immediately dissipates.

A stroke of lightning reveals a candle on a nearby table. Alongside it is a small wooden container with matches. He takes one stick and lights the candle. The candle's flickering flames provide a dim but welcome refuge from the total darkness. The young boy steps into the large Buddha hall.

"Grandfather," calls Daiki in a soft voice, while holding the candle higher, moving it across his path of vision where he can see the temple's entryway to the front as well as his grandfather's living quarters off to one side. Daiki turns toward the quarters, passing through a living room and a dining area.

"Amazing! Absolutely, remarkably amazing! This is exactly as I remember it. Nothing has changed."

Daiki notices that dinner plates on the dining table have been set for a meal that's never eaten. Not only has the temple apparently been deserted, it has also been abandoned in a hurry.

Carrying the candle, Daiki wanders through the familiar rooms of his past, searching for clues to the temple's condition and his grandfather's sudden disappearance. He finds his old bedroom strangely undisturbed like that of his Grandfather's. As he moves toward the main temple area and steps into the opening of the larger room, a brilliant flash of lightning reveals the figure of a large man walking past the outside windows.

Cautiously, the young Japanese moves closer to the temple's front entryway. He peers through one side of the left window but can see no one. The cryptic figure has disappeared. Daiki moves slowly toward the door and crosses in front of the window. He removes his yo-yo and positions himself near the doorway. Waiting. Listening.

Another brilliant flash of lightning, accompanied by loud clap of thunder, blends with the smashing sound of the front door as it bursts open. The huge figure of a man emerges through the door, his arm swinging in a swift downward path toward Daiki.

Daiki steps aside, barely missing the sharp blow as it pounds through the air, which otherwise would have been his arm. Confused and hesitant, he refuses to give way to panic. In Daiki's moment of hesitation, however, the man executes a powerful roundhouse kick to Daiki's stomach, drops to the floor where he follows with a spinning back-kick to Daiki's face.

The young Japanese is unable to block the man's powerful kicks and is sent flying to the farthermost corner of the room. The room's darkness and the surprised attack by the mysterious assailant unnerves Daiki who brings his focus to bear in order to control both his breathing and fear. He remembers his grandfather's admonition about being scared after the fact, and in the process also recalls his advice with regard to darkness.

"Do not try to see with your eyes in total darkness, but instead open your eyes in your mind."

Daiki immediately closes his eyes and breathes slowly and deeply which enables him to become better aware of his surroundings. The more Daiki relaxes himself, the more he can see what is around him. Breathing deeply once again, he takes an oblique martial arts' "Hanmi" stance, with his arms spread wide as though he's going to hug someone. His pose becomes calm and natural.

The assailant, now moving aggressively forward, appears to be aware of his opponent's change of nature. It's the assailant who now hesitates.

Through his mind's eyes, Daiki is able to feel his opponent's presence. The young man's ears have become increasingly more sensitive so that a tiny drop of water can be heard dripping from the faucet in the kitchen.

Again, the assailant rushes toward Daiki who is able to sense where the movement is coming from. Daiki feels that he is in the presence of an expert martial artist, but that he has no choice but to overcome the situation and to win the battle at hand. He shifts his right foot slightly and pretends to cross his left foot. Instead, he spins his body 90 degrees, in a semi-circle, to his right, and at the same time, rotates on his left foot and with the opposite foot places a spinning back-kick to his opponent. The assailant, however, easily blocks Daiki's kick, causing him to kick the air in vain and without contact.

Unhesitatingly, Daiki follows with multiple punches and kick combinations. However, the assailant's blocks are so smooth, flexible, and effective that Daiki senses that he is fighting against the atmosphere.

Daiki spins and kicks high, but the man catches his kick, grasps his leg, and shoves his body upward. He flies though the air, but manages to somersault in mid-air and land on the floor, while his assailant grabs one a heavy broomstick that leans against the temple wall.

The smooth, sneaky assailant moves forward, executes a spinning assault, using the wooden shaft. For the first time, Daiki is able to use his Yo-Yo as a direct parry to the swinging rod. The whirling object unwinds from the metal chord, striking the pole and knocking it away. The Yo-Yo quickly recoils but Daiki loses no time casting it out once again.

The room brightens momentarily as a flash of lightening explodes across the sky.

**DAIKI USES HIS YO-YO AS A DIRECT PARRY
TO THE SWINGING ROD.**

The lightning flash briefly highlights the spiraling Yo-Yo as it twirls toward Daiki's forward-rushing enemy. It strikes his opponent's shoulder and causes the man to spin away and absorbs the pounding shock of the metal object.

For a fleeting moment, another lightning streak brightens the room. Suddenly, the assailant stops and retreats to the deep shadows just outside the open door frame. He breathes sharply as he speaks.

"Daiki?"

Daiki, also breathing heavily, strains to see who the foreboding figure is. A bolt of lightning ignites the sky behind the man and reveals the face of the assailant.

Daiki gasps, takes several steps backward before throwing down his weapon. Framed by the open door, another bolt of lightning illuminates and reveals the face of Daiki's assailant.

"Grandfather!" bellows the young boy.

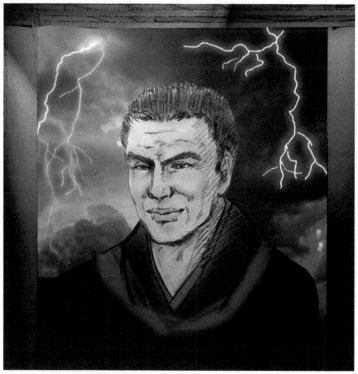

A BOLT OF LIGHTNING IGNITES THE SKY BEHIND THE MAN AND REVEALS THE FACE OF HIS ATTACKER.

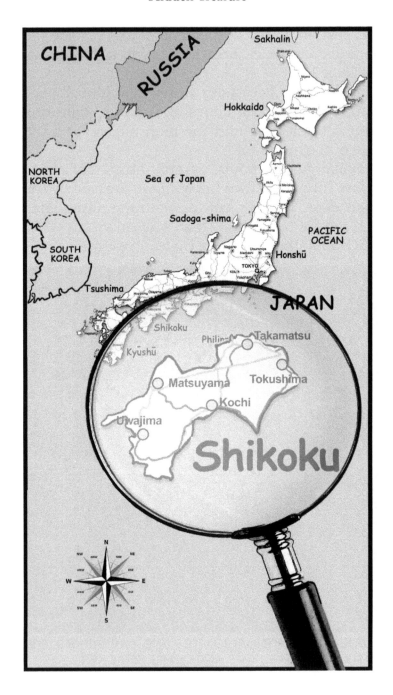

HIDDEN TREASURE
Chapter Twelve

"**G**RANDFATHER?" IMPLORES DAIKI. "Is that you?"

The unrecognizable dark shadow pauses and cautiously asks in return, "Daiki?"

A brilliant flash of lightning illuminates both silhouettes that reveals Daiki and Grandfather Daichi facing close to each other.

Both drop their guard and fall into each other's arms. The grandfather, overcome with emotion, weeps unabashedly.

"I did not recognize you. Many have broken into this temple. Had I not seen the Yin-Yang medallion, I could have killed you."

Then suddenly, Daichi's mood changes; his face becomes dark and brooding. The abrupt change in his grandfather's countenance startles Daiki who finds himself staring into those dark eyes that are both uncompromising and inflexible.

"Grandfather . . . ?"

"Why are you here?" demands the grandfather. "Why have you come to Japan?"

"I had no choice. A fellow student at the university was killed and another badly injured – here on Shikoku – near my home! The professor who brought them here was also killed. Four others are . . ."

"You have disobeyed my wishes," interrupts the older man. "You came despite my precise instructions for you to do otherwise."

"I could do nothing else, Grandfather. You should know Prof. Thompson saved my life in Los Angeles. I declined his offer to accompany him on this trip, free all the way. Had I done so, perhaps the professor would not have been killed. That is why I feel partly responsible for his sudden death . . . this is a grave matter of honor and reputation." Grandfather Daichi says nothing, but his expression belies the fact that he knows his grandson is telling the truth.

"But I do not care about my reputation," continues Daiki, "for it is merely what others know of me. However, you always have me to care for honor, because honor is what we know of ourselves. Coming here to Shikoku after Prof. Thompson's death is a matter of honor, nothing else."

Another bright streak of lightning shines over the grandfather's face. But when the light fades, Daiki finds himself facing a tall and dark frightening figure--one whom he feels he has never known before.

After what seems like an eternity, the changed dark figure of the grandfathers speaks, "So now, have you completed your journey?"

"No, Grandfather. You taught me that when ninety percent of a journey is complete, I am only half way there."

"Come with me," orders the grandfather. "We must talk."

Daiki follows his grandfather from the main floor to the living quarters to the left side of the temple. The older man abruptly stops and turns toward his grandson, strikes a match, and crosses his arm toward a large candle, and lights it. The flickering candlelight casts strange, terrifying shadows across the grandfather's face.

"Sit down," sternly orders Daichi.

"WE MUST TALK," SAYS THE GRANDFATHER.

Daiki and his grandfather take a seat at a dining room table in the temple's living quarters. The room is lit only by the iridescent glow of three large candles, enough light for Daiki and his grandfather to see each other. Beyond that, the little light reaches the strange, dark, and ominous interior of the temple where shadows seem to flicker, appear, then fade. Daiki tries anxiously not to further upset the older man.

"I had to come, Grandfather. The two who were killed were my friends; the other one is still hospitalized."

"Humm," grumbles Daichi, eyeing his

grandson closely. "A girl, I presume?"

Daiki swallows hard, then nods, thinking that there is very little he can offer as an excuse. His grandfather goes on with his admonition.

"Ten years have passed and I have not heard from you. Not once. Not one letter came from you, not even one!" says the older man almost breathlessly.

"I...I wanted to. I was . . ."

Daichi angrily interrupts, "The only news I ever heard about you came from Mr. Sasaki. Still, I continue to send you money . . . to see that you are cared for. Now, you show up unexpectedly, against my explicit wishes. Is this how you show gratitude?"

"Grandfather, I was upset as well. Please try to understand. I was very young when you forced me to leave my home. My parents had just been killed and I had no time to even grieve. And before I knew it, I was in a foreign country with strangers--with no explanation whatsoever. Nothing--just this--this medallion. And I didn't understand what that was about, either."

Daichi draws a deep breath, his anger a bit subsiding. "My only consideration at the time was for your safety. You could not stay here."

"Grandfather, I was eight years old then."

The grandfather says nothing more nor does his expression change. He pauses for a long time and silently watches his grandson. This makes Daiki even more uncomfortable. Finally, Daichi breaks the long silence.

"You have changed. You have lost the way of

the Shugendo. You were taught strength through hardship; obedience through practice; and discipline through the study of the flow of water. But look at you, now. America has made you soft!"

A moment passes without any further word from either one. Daiki stares at the ground, avoiding the glare of his grandfather's ire. Then he looks up and, without a blink in his eyes, unflinchingly and determinedly replies.

"I did not come to quarrel with you, Grandfather. I am here because . . . because you are the only person who can help me. So many strange things have happened to me recently. No! More than strange. They are bizarre events, unreasonably out-of-this-world, inexplicable, incomprehensible even, if I may say."

Daiki pulls a case from his backpack and from it retrieves the Kukai scroll and hands it to his grandfather.

"Please, Grandfather. Look at this. I think it belonged to . . ."

Before Daiki can say anything else, Daichi demands, "Where did you get this? Who gave it to you?"

"It was left by Prof. Thompson, the teacher who was killed in the accident."

The grandfather, in visibly extreme anger, stands and storms about the room, gathering his thoughts. All too suddenly, he whips around, turning on Daiki and exclaims, "I do not want to discuss this any further!"

"But, Grandfather, I need your help," Daiki pleads.

"What is it about what I have said that you do

not understand?" yells Daichi, his voice rising. "I will speak of this no longer, and neither will you."

"YOUR MEETING WAS A disaster, I can tell," says Jun sympathetically. "I'm very sorry."

Daiki sits on the edge of Jun's bed. A nurse completes her medical notes that are on a metal clipboard which she places in a holder at the foot of the bed before stepping out of the room.

"Disaster is an understatement, Jun. I asked him for help and he refused to discuss what I need. He was aloof, cold, and distant--even when I told him of your accident."

"I guess that's it then, huh!" sighs Jun.

Daiki pauses for a while, a look of determination crossing his face, "On the contrary. This just means that we will, and must, solve the scroll's mystery ourselves, without his help."

The two are interrupted by a knock at the door and by Steve's bursting into the room.

"We're waiting for you, Daiki," he says.

"Thanks, Steve. I'll be right there." Turning to Jun, Daiki continues, "I have to go, but I'll see you tomorrow. You have my number, call me if you need anything."

Steve glances at Jun's bedside, and notices Jun's holding Daiki's hand.

"Be careful," urges Jun, "I cannot explain it, but something seems very wrong."

"I will. Don't worry," responds Daiki as he

releases Jun's hand.

"Come on, Steve. Let's go."

She watches as the two leave the room. An orderly comes in behind them.

"Time for your meal, Miss Lee."

Just as Daiki and Steve are leaving the hospital; they see a black Mitsubishi Galant heading toward them in the parking lot. The vehicle pulls into a vacant spot beside Daiki's rented yellow Honda. Capt. Sato steps from his car, quizzically looks at them, and bows, with his hand strangely behind him, as though trying to conceal something.

"Is this a coincidence or predestination?" asks Sato mockingly.

Daiki and Steve as well as the rest of the group are caught off guard. They are not expecting to see the police captain, especially one smiling as broadly as he is. The captain reacts to their body language.

"I mean; I arrive just as all of you are leaving. A coincidence, don't you think? Or is it, really?"

Without blinking or saying anything, Capt. Sato stares directly at Daiki.

It is an awkward moment of silence for all of them until Capt. Sato says, "I don't believe that we have met," directly addressing Daiki.

Daiki is unsure of what to say; William catches the drift, steps in, and answers, "This is a friend of ours from the States. Daiki Ike. He is here to see Jun . . . Miss Lee."

Capt. Sato turns toward William, again silent and unblinking. This time it's William who fidgets. Capt. Sato turns toward Daiki, slightly bows, and says, "Ah, I understand. Mr. Ike, that's an uncommon name."

"It is," immediately replies Daiki, but says nothing more.

Capt. Sato nods. "I am pleased to meet you then, Mr. Ike," and continues to address all the students.

"How are you spending your leisure time now that you have abandoned your temple trip?" Without waiting for a reply from the students, Capt. Sato answers his own question.

"Waiting around for something to happen, I presume." No one gives the captain a reply; everyone remains quiet. "I suspect it must be rather dull for you," Capt. Sato adds.

Daiki takes a half-step forward and somewhat aggressively asks, "Is this an official call?"

"Official? Oh! No, no, no! I didn't mean to imply that. I am not here on business," Capt. Sato says defensively, and now shows off what he seems to hide behind his back--a colorful red posy flower. Jose and William breathe a sigh of relief that a flower is all that the captain is carrying. William has been thinking it may have been a firearm; he is now even more relieved.

Jose looks furtively in Daiki's direction, but gets more nervous when he notices that Capt. Sato is aware of the glances he has just made.

"Oh," says Sato lifting the flower slightly, "This is for Miss Lee. I have come to wish her a speedy recovery." Smiling an emotionless smile, "This is one of the more pleasant parts of my duties."

Capt. Sato starts to walk away but abruptly stops and turns toward the group.

"I understand that you are moving into a new

hotel?"

All that William can do is manage a weak, sheepish smile.

"Well," says Sato, half-smiling again. "I can hardly blame you, considering your last accommodations were, shall we say, Spartan."

Without waiting for an answer but relishing the student's uncomfortable situation with all the questions he has asked them, Capt. Sato bows, turns, and finally hurriedly walks away.

"Come on," Daiki urges everybody, "Let's get out of here."

THE RYOKAN INN IS a small lodging located deep within an isolated mountainous region of Shikoku. It has a two-story rustic building with sixteen Tatami rooms, and a single three-story structure built atop its midsection is used as a dining area. The building, constructed mostly of wood, is painted in contrasting gold and brown. A country-rock ledge, erected adjacent to the inn, serves as a ground retainer and runs a few hundred feet up until it meets the mountainside. In the front is a parking area where only Daiki's vehicle rests.

Daiki and William are the first ones to get out of the car, with Violet, Jose, and Steve following behind.

"Not many guests, it seems," says Steve.

"The place is rustic, that's for sure," quipped William.

THE RYOKAN INN IS A SMALL LODGING LOCATED DEEP WITHIN AN ISOLATED MOUNTAINOUS REGION OF SHIKOKU.

"Kind of small," says Violet. "I wonder if they have hot-and-cold running water!"

"Of course," replies Daiki. "You'll find that the owners are a charming couple and their place is very quiet. I think we'll get more done in here."

"With no Capt. Sato around to make us nervous," adds William.

Daiki opens the trunk, and each one grabs his/her own luggage. "Come on," says Daiki. "Let's check in and go to our own rooms. We can check out the dining room as well. I'm told it's kind of small, but larger than any other rooms should we need more space to meet and lay everything out and work."

The students sign in and with their luggage go up to the second-story. They reach the hallway and stop by the door outside their respective room, while Daiki unlocks and opens his.

"Here we are," says Daiki. "Violet, you're in the room next door."

"Lucky you," says William. "You avoid the unpleasant smells."

"Cripes!" exclaims Jose. "Talk about smells. Have you checked yourself lately?'"

The room is small with eight Tatami mats and a small table that sits under a window-unit air-conditioner. Everyone throws his/her bags on the floor and looks around. Steve is the first to say something.

"It's cool outside, so we probably won't need the air-conditioners."

"You're kidding!" retorts William who's short of breath for carrying the equipment. "Those are some elevators . . ."

"There're no elevators," says Steve.

"That's what I mean," replies William. "Those are some elevators!"

The others laugh. Daiki begins setting up a computer and video monitors.

"I want you to look at a few things before you settle in," reminds Daiki while he quickly connects his MacBook-Pro to a double set of screens and a printer. He places a portable makeshift whiteboard to the side along with some colored markers.

"Okay, guys, you know about Kukai from your classes," says Daiki. "You'll remember that in his time, he was the most celebrated monk in Japanese history."

"Yeah, yeah, yeah," interrupts Steve in a slightly hostile tone. "We've gone over all of this in class."

"I'm going over it again because it's important to our task and it's the reason for our being here."

"He's on target, Steve," says William. "Quiet down for a minute and let him finish. Go ahead, Daiki."

"What you don't know is what that radio commentator back in L.A. used to call, 'the rest of the story.' One day, Japan's Emperor Saga summoned Kukai to the royal court where he was then carried by palanquin to the Emperor's palace."

"What's a palanquin?" asks Violet.

"It's an open-seated box that's carried by four or more servants, usually with two or three on each side. Only very special people rode this way and it was by this means that the highly respected Kukai was brought to the Emperor."

"Anyway, here he is, a civil servant, a poet, scholar, and artist. Even with all his achievements, he's in awe that he has been asked to such a magnificent palace."

"You see, Emperor Saga was resigning and it was his desire to leave his immense treasure to his subjects, the people of Japan. He wanted it available to them for their use in case of the very worst of emergencies."

"What kind of emergencies?" Jose asks.

"Famines, earthquakes, even an occasional

tsunami. Japan, being an island nation, was and still is, always subject to these calamities."

"And back then," interrupts Steve, "There were no early warnings."

"Steve is right," says Daiki. "Kukai was the only person whom the Emperor felt was qualified enough to handle the treasure. He needed someone who was not only qualified but also trustworthy."

"Where was the treasure kept?" asks Violet.

"The Emperor kept it near himself, in the palace. He showed Kukai the treasure's location which was in a secret cavern behind a huge iron door."

"Does anyone know what has happened to it?" asks William.

"Yes, sort of," replies Daiki. "Kukai supervised the transfer of the treasure aboard the Emperor's ship from the palace."

Daiki pauses briefly in his retelling the story, which builds the tension up in the room. As the silence continues, Violet interrupts.

"Okay, so what happened?"

"I don't know. No one does. It was the last time the Emperor and Kukai ever saw each other. In time, the treasure became subject of wild rumors and the rumors became myths. Finally, the treasure just became a dying Japanese legend."

"Okay. But, I'm not following this," declares Steve.

"Yeah, neither am I," says Jose.

Daiki walks to the whiteboard and picks up a black marker and draws a makeshift image of Japan. He labels the country, and in smaller letters drops to the lower southwest area of Japan and labels the island of Shikoku. Next he removes the scroll from its case.

"Here's what we've learned. Kukai drew this scroll, which remained hidden for very long. Now, where did he live? Here, on Shikoku," says Daiki pointing to the map. "I believe that he came directly to Shikoku from the emperor's palace."

"Because . . .?" inquires Steve.

"Because Shikoku was the one place that Kukai knew better than anyone else. He knew its forests, creeks, rivers, and especially its mountains, like no one else did. In other words, if anyone knew where to hide a treasure on Shikoku, it was Kukai."

"I'm beginning to like Prof. Thompson's class more and more," says Steve.

"The heck with Thompson's class," replies William. "I'm just glad that Daiki is here when we need him."

Daiki looks sad and says, "I'm sorry I wasn't here sooner when the professor needed my help . . . when he asked for my help."

"Yeah, well you're here now and that's what's important," catches Violet. "And I know Jun is happy about it."

Daiki looks rather surprised at Violet, his whole face asking for confirmation.

"Because she told me so, silly."

Steve scowls, but no one pays attention. All the talk of treasure, the scroll, and map, has the group get even more excited.

"Well, you're here now and we're with you Daiki," says Jose. "But the question is, how are we going to find the treasure on Shikoku? This is such a big island."

Daiki re-rolls the scroll, holds it up, and declares, "The secret treasure is buried here in this island--somewhere here, somewhere!"

Steve steps forward and impatiently says, "All right then, let's not stop; let's keep on moving. Let's get back to work!"

"Not stop?" quips William. "I'm hungry."

"So am I," adds Violet. "We haven't eaten since breakfast."

"And I missed that," adds William.

"You said this place has a diner," says Steve pointing at Daiki.

"Upstairs," replies Daiki.

"Okay, then," says Steve. "Let's take what we have with us. We can eat while we work. You happy now, William?"

William smiles.

"Good idea," says Daiki. "I'll print off what I've copied from the scroll so we have more to work with. Go ahead and put your stuff away in your room, guys. Violet, your room is adjacent to mine. We'll meet in the diner in about thirty minutes, maybe?"

A short while later the group has moved upstairs to the inn's small but attractive dining room. They seem to be the only guests at the inn because no one else has come to eat there. William and Jose put two benches together so everyone can sit together while eating and studying Daiki's printed material at the same time.

Each of them has a copy of the writings along with the star diagram that Daiki has copied from the scroll. Taped to one side of the whiteboard is a printed blowup of the same diagram.

Steve, William, and Daiki have made translations of the scroll's Japanese text into English so that everyone can read the manuscript. Violet has been doing just that when she asks, "What does Kukai mean when he writes, 'the deeper, something or other stuff'?"

"I believe it's this," says Daiki, reading from the scroll. "'The deeper the thought, the deeper the confusion'. What he's saying is that perhaps the information on the scroll isn't enough to solve the puzzle."

"I'm okay guys," says Violet. "Really! Just get me another cup of tea or strong coffee."

I'll get it," quickly responds Jose, "and one for me as well. Anybody else?"

"I'm okay," replies Daiki.

"I'm not," says William. "Make mine coffee and black."

"Steve?"

"No, I'm fine, Jose. Thanks."

Jose proceeds to the opposite end of the diner where both coffee and tea are brewing.

"Back to the drawing board, everyone. Let's go at this again," directs Daiki. "Tomorrow morning first thing, we need to pay the local library a visit. This is going to take a lot more work."

"THE CHINESE CHARACTER ON THE TOP MEANS WOOD, SAYS DAIKI. "THE SYMBOL TO THE LEFT IS EARTH. OPPOSITE IT, ON THE RIGHT, IS METAL. MOVE TO THE BOTTOM LEFT AND THE FIGURE IS WATER. OPPOSITE IT IS FIRE."

With a faint sigh, the group returns to give the diagram another look and begins to study it again.

RISING EARLY AHEAD OF his friends, Daiki drives to his grandfather's temple. He leaves his car nearby and walks through the early morning shadows, from the temple to the tombstones of his father, mother, and grandmother. The morning sun is barely up and with the grey foggy mist rising, the pathway looks dark and ominous, making the trek even more foreboding. But Daiki knows the pathway all too well.

Daiki stops when he reaches his family's tombstones, drops to his knees, bows his head, and begins to pray. There is sadness in the tone of his spoken Japanese. One doesn't have to understand the language to realize that someone is under a great deal of stress. And Daiki is!

The fog continues to thicken, such that the temple in the background can barely be seen. However dimly, the outline of a figure emerges in the shadows of a recess in the temple's façade, and moves forward only to blend with a nearby clump of red maple trees.

Sensing something, but not knowing what it is, Daiki glances up. Seeing nothing, he turns to finish his prayers. As he prays, the sinister figure re-emerges and moves toward him. Daiki looks up again, but sees only the swirling midst in the early morning shadows. Still, something tells him to stay alert and be more keen and aware. He is staring toward the temple and vainly trying to peer through the dense fog when he suddenly spots a dark figure passing from one patch of shadows only to disappear abruptly into another.

Daiki stands, looks around, and listens carefully before proceeding toward the temple. A moment later, he sees the spook emerge from the mist and vanish around the corner of the temple. Daiki quickens his pace, his senses mindful as he approaches the temple columns. There is no one in sight.

Flattening himself against the wall, Daiki eases himself slowly toward the back of the temple. As he cautiously rounds the corner, heavy ropes fall about him. For a moment, he is startled but then realizes they are not ropes but heavy vines overgrown from the years of over-growth.

"Control Daiki," he whispers to himself. "Calm. Be calm as a peaceful lake, not turbulent like the waterfall." Then, looking upward, he gets an idea.

Grabbing hold of the vines, he quickly scales to the top of the temple and quietly runs along the ridge until he reaches the very front of the temple. Peering down, he sees a figure of a man disappear into the swirling fog. Daiki drops silently to the ground and moves toward where he thinks the man is. Then, instantly, he feels that as he follows his quarry, he is also being followed.

Daiki walks evasively into a shadowy mist, vanishing from sight. He hears approaching footsteps that make him move farther back into his cover waiting for the right moment. As he does so, he is grabbed by a stout shadowy figure.

"Don't move," orders the phantom-like shape. "You are being followed."

Daiki is pulled farther into the shadowy mist of yellow fog. Strong, solid arms hold him tightly, and when he tries to cry out, a heavy hand across his lips immediately silences him.

"Shhh," comes the whisper. "Be silent."

He turns his head and recognizes his grandfather. Daiki relaxes as the older man murmurs in an even lower voice, "Stay here.

There is an imminent danger. Let me deal with this," says the grandfather who vanishes as quickly as he has appeared.

Daiki, left standing by himself, senses that the entire situation is bizarre and weird. Even what his grandfather has told him sounds suspicious. He can wait only a moment longer and then proceeds to follow in the direction that his grandfather has taken. He crosses the garden toward the temple, gets there, and then edges his way around the corner where he has seen his grandfather disappear again.

Carefully, Daiki peers around the corner but sees . . . nothing. The phantom figure is gone as well as his grandfather!

**THE PHANTOM FIGURE IS GONE...
AS WELL AS HIS GRANDFATHER!**

KUKAI AND HIS HANGING SCROLL

KUKAI'S SECRET
Chapter Thirteen

CARRYING AN ARMLOAD OF books and papers, Steve leaves the local village library. He recognizes Daiki crossing the street in his direction and loses no time calling him.

"Hey, Daiki! I've found an entire Kukai collection of books. I'm ready to do more research on his treasure. Are you heading back to the inn now?"

"Not just yet," yells back Daiki. "I want to check on Jun and see how she's doing. Where are the others?"

"Jose and Violet are researching in the library; the older books and documents, by the way, are hard to find. It's tough to check out anything without a library card. Good thing I have an international student card, but I did register for a card there. You can't believe the size of the deposit I had to leave behind just to borrow what I did. But I have discovered that we wouldn't be able to remove the older stuff at all."

"I understand, Steve. That's okay; we'll go back to the library to study what we have to, if we need to."

"Without the older documents will surely hamper our search, I would think," grunts Steve.

"I have another idea," adds Daiki. "Go back to the Tenkai-ji Temple; ancient shrines and temples often have archives. Maybe they'll let you search through them."

"Good idea. I'll head for there now. I can look later over these books I've checked out."

"I'll get Jose and Violet," says Daiki. "They can ride with me back to the inn. William is still there working with the numbers. When you finish at the temple, grab a taxi and join us."

"Got it. See you back at the base."

Daiki nods while Steve hustles off. From where the two are, an ominous figure passes by very slowly in a black Nissan-Centra and snaps a photograph of Daiki who's hopping into his yellow rental Honda. The ill-boding stranger smiles faintly then drives away.

Reaching the temple by taxi, Steve makes his way to its archives where books and scrolls on specialized religious literature line the walls. An aging monk, looking much older than the antique furniture in the office, attempts to help him.

"The book you're looking for no longer exists. The only copy we had has been missing for many years now," says the monk with a hint of distrust in his voice.

"Are you sure?" asks Steve probingly.

"Young man," answers the monk. "I know when a volume is available and when it is not. I have been here more than fifty years, and in all that time you are the only person who ever asked for it. Then, looking at Steve suspiciously, the monk asks, "Did you say that you were a student-scholar?"

"Well, not exactly. But I am doing a paper on Kukai. That is, I mean . . ."

"In that case, you are in the wrong place, Mr. Chan," says the monk dismissively. "I recommend that you begin with Kukai's poetry. You will find a volume at the visitor bookstore by the temple entrance . . . on your way out!"

Steve sighs, bows slightly, and then leaves. "Oh, that didn't go well!" he says to himself. "What to do, what to do?"

"WHEN WILL THEY LET you out of here, Jun?" asks Daiki while nervously flicking his yo-yo medallion down, up, and then back again.

"Sometime tomorrow," replies Jun. "I feel fine, but they want to do more tests."

"When they let you out, I'll be here to pick you up."

"Thank you, but if you're busy at the inn, I can take a taxi."

"No, I want to pick you up!" blurts Daiki who, upon realizing what he says and how he says it, feels his face turning red.

"That's nice. I would like for you to," says Jun with a smile on her lips.

"Settled then. Now we just have to find out when they'll let you go. Violet has her own room at the inn, so there's plenty of space for you there."

A tall Asian man, in a long white doctor's coat, walks in all the way to the end of the bed and lifts Jun's clipboard from its holder.

"This is my doctor," says Jun in a soft whisper. "Let's ask him. Dr. Watanabe!"

"Yes," replies Watanabe, glancing up from the chart.

"This is my boyfriend, Daiki Ike," who blushes at Jun's unexpected declaration.

"He's asking when I may be released."

Watanabe bows slightly, smiling as he answers. "Everything looks fine on the charts. Nothing was broken, but you were unconscious for a long time. We need to keep you under observation, but I expect we can let you go in the morning."

"That's good news, indeed," says Jun. "Thank you, doctor."

"You're very welcome," replies Dr. Watanabe who makes a few more notes on the chart. "I will see you tomorrow then." He clips back the pen into his front coat pocket and walks away.

Jun turns to Daiki, "Okay now, you were telling me that you guys have been steadily working on the Kukai problem."

"We have," says Daiki, spinning his yo-yo in a new direction. "The complexity of it all is maddening. William and I have been at it since early this morning. I've made a series of numerical calculations—set after set--and all that the computer does is spew out a great deal more numbers that require more and more computations."

"Of course, you understand them," Jun says.

Daiki shakes his head sideways, meaning no.

"Can't the others help?" asks Jun. Daiki negatively shakes his head sideways.

"Really, not all. But William is good on computers and his Harvard experience proves helpful. I left him at the inn to run more computations and to print out what we have. They should be ready when I get back."

Daiki continues to spin his yo-yo up and down absentmindedly. Even though he pays no attention to it, Jun does.

"What is that?" she asks. "You always have it with you. It looks like a yo-yo, but seems heavier . . . different!"

"It's a metal trinket of some kind that my grandfather gave me – a medallion of sorts."

"IT'S A METAL TRINKET OF SOME KIND THAT MY GRANDFATHER GAVE ME – A MEDALLION OF SORTS."

"It's unusual. May I see it?"

"Sure, here," replies Daiki, rewinding the yo-yo and handing it to her.

"It's funny looking for a yo-yo," observes Jun.

"It wasn't always a yo-yo," Daiki tries to explain.

"No?"

"No. I added the steel cord. The medallion is heavy and a regular string wouldn't work. Don't know why I still carry it around . . . just do. Still, it has come in handy every now and then."

"This symbol on each side, I recognize it," says Jun. "It's the Yin-Yang!"

"Yes, that's what I thought, too," replies Daiki. "I know it has to do with opposites of some kind, but what? I know very little about it."

"The Yin and Yang represent opposite forces," Jun says, "but they are really complementary."

"My grandfather talked about it when I was a little boy. He referred to the two sides as the enmity and affinity."

"What did he mean by that?" asks Jun.

"Enmity is combative and pushes away. Affinity is empathetic and attracts."

"The Yin and Yang," says Jun. "Together these opposite forces in the world of elements are actually complementary."

"Exactly. Wood can break earth and water can cover earth," adds Daiki.

"Right, water puts out fire, but fire evaporates the water." Jun continues, "The fire can melt metal and we have come full circle, because metal can cut earth, but dulls itself in the process."

"And these are the five elements that are also referred to in Kukai's puzzle," Daiki says.

"Let's be sure we have the big picture in all of this," says Jun. "Wood helps fire to burn, while the fire makes ashes to form the earth. The earth forms metals, metals hold water, and water makes the trees grow, which is the wood."

"Very good, Jun!" Daiki agrees. "It's yet another way of looking at how it works. Hey, you've become a sage yourself, Jun. Each element helps support another relationship in nature."

"And it is that relationship in nature that is the Yin and Yang!" she exclaims.

"There you go," says Daiki laughing. "I think we've got it."

"So this is how opposites attract," smiles Jun sweetly, placing her hand on Daiki's as she gives the yo-yo back to him. Daiki can only feel his face blushing red again.

"Yin and Yang," Jun continues. "That's what you have with your grandfather."

"How's that?" Daiki asks further.

"You two are opposites. He's enmity and you're affinity. You are both family and you should be complementary and supportive, but neither of you are."

"Forget about that," Daiki replies. "My grandfather isn't that way. He doesn't intend to help me, much less help us. Even worse, he's devious and uncommunicative. He is convinced that I am hiding something from him. After what happened at his temple, I will probably never see him again." Jun doesn't answer right away as though lost in thought.

"You are seeing this only one way, the Yin. Perhaps, there is another way, the Yang," Jun almost hesitantly adds. Daiki looks at Jun, puzzled by her statement.

"Perhaps, it is your grandfather who is trying to hide something from you," Jun continues.

Daiki considers what Jun has just said, appropriately sensing something more ominous. He says nothing more. And Jun, still keeping her hand over his, leans over and kisses him tenderly on the cheek.

JUN, KEEPING HER HAND OVER HIS, LEANS OVER AND KISSES HIM TENDERLY ON THE CHEEK.

DAIKI EXPLAINS THE COMPLEXITY OF KUKAI'S RANDOM NUMBERS

NIGHT SHADOWS
Chapter Fourteen

STEVE, VIOLET, AND JOSE have returned to the inn earlier and are working with William when Daiki, coming back from the hospital, joins them. Together, they have converted Daiki's room into a battle station. What furniture there was before has been shoved—along with the tatami mats--to the side of the room. Daiki's entire computer system is assembled against a wall adjacent to the door; the two large monitors filled with research data are placed on a long table that has been removed from the inn's dining area. On the wall, next to the windows hangs an oversized reprinted copies and diagrams of calculations William and Daiki have made, along with all the information collected by the others. In the middle of the wall is Kukai's cryptic star that has been printed extra-large and now is the centerpiece of the wall, if not of the entire room.

All five of them--Daiki, Steve, William, Jose, and Violet--are fully discussing the enigmatic star when Daiki and William suddenly and unexpectedly begin to speak in Japanese. Steve, Violet, and Jose look at one another and then try to listen to the Japanese-language, two-person conversation, which none of them has no way of understanding, try as they may.

"Excuse me," interrupts Jose. Getting no response, he tries once more, this time a little louder.

"Guys--Steve, Violet, and I cannot understand a single word you both are saying."

"Oh, sorry about that," says Daiki. "It just seems easier to converse in my native language."

"Well, not so easy for me," admits William, "but at least I was able to understand Daiki when he started off in his native language."

"Here's what we're saying," says Daiki apologetically. "This entire scroll, the mystery scroll, all of it was created by Kukai with one purpose in mind."

"Which was?" asks Jose.

"Which was to record what happened to the treasure and, more importantly, where it is," says Daiki. Without losing a beat, William adds, "You see, we have figured out that if you read Kukai's star clockwise, you come up with a series of numbers . . . that must mean something."

"That's why we have translated the Japanese numbers into Arabic, so that you guys can understand them."

"You must be kidding!" blurts Violet. "I still don't understand any of it."

"Of course, not," says Daiki. "They are random numbers doing what they're supposed to do."

"Which is?" asks Steve who's trying to understand it all.

"Confuse you! Us!" replies Daiki.

"They're doing that all right," agrees Steve.

"Focus for a minute on the star," says Daiki. "Three concentric circles, made up of numbers, surround it. Starting with the word wood and then moving clockwise, we see the numbers 10-- 6 – 7; going past metal to 10 – 5 – 6; passing fire and moving on we come to 3 – 10 – 10; passing water and so on until we reach the 'Kou' symbol before the word earth. Beneath this circle of numbers is a second inner circle, and below that is another, smaller one, each with a specific series of numbers. They must mean something, but we don't know what it is, just yet."

"It's puzzling, huh? And that is just a clockwise reading," says William. "When you move counter clockwise, immediately you generate an entirely different set of numbers."

"Or you can go clockwise on one circle, counter clockwise on the second, and clockwise again on the third," Daiki adds.

"Yep," declares William, "or you can do the same thing backwards. You could even take the numbers in stacks. For instance, look at the number printed to the right of wood. It reads 10 – 5 –, and then 'Kou'."

"Aarrggg," screams Violet. You're driving me nuts. What are you talking about?"

"Brilliant," replies Daiki, returning to the star centered in the wall of numbers. "I said it before: Kukai didn't want us to figure this out and that is why he used an infinite set of random numbers."

"So it's these random numbers that you've plastered all over the wall?" asks Steve.

"Exactly," replies William.

"What we are trying to do," says Daiki, "is to make sense of what the star's integers mean. Look at the arbitrary Chinese characters surrounding the scroll. There's an infinite possibility of varying interpretations. Yet the Chinese character--'Kou'--remains an odd ball that throws our calculations off by seemingly having no pattern at all."

"Even when we look at the star from a counter clockwise direction, the Chinese 'Kou' pops up routinely, but in unexpected places," continues Daiki.

"Yep. No pattern and we haven't even started calculating the two inner circle numbers," says William in agreement.

Jose and Violet have blank looks on their faces. Daiki and William look at each other, confident that they have lost their friends in the discussion, even when speaking in English.

"Let's face it. This isn't going to be easy. The smartest man in Japan intentionally made this impossibly difficult," says Daiki.

"Yeah, and he's up there now laughing at us," adds William!

"I'm missing the joke!" interjects Violet. Daiki pauses for a moment before pasting a large sheet of butcher paper on the wall.

"This is what we know at this very moment: all of the calculations that we have so far made mean nothing. So, let's start all over again."

Groans instantaneously rise from around the room.

NIGHT SHADOWS FLIRT WITH the dim lights in the darkened hallways of the hospital. An orderly, passing from one room to the next and checking its occupants, stops abruptly. One of the shadows appears to be in motion. The ward attendant pauses as he peers into the darkness and tries to focus on the living shadow. Seeing nothing, he continues to another room.

The mysterious shadow moves again, gliding from one patch of darkness to another. Cloaked in sheer blackness, it slithers and floats along the shadowy corridors. As it nears a set of doors that leads to another section of the hospital, the ingress opens, allowing the shadow to pass through. And then, as quickly as it appears, it is suddenly gone.

Dr. Watanabe sets his medical notes aside on a desk, removes his white coat and hangs it on a clothes tree in one corner of the office. He takes his cell phone from the coat's pocket and dials a number.

Speaking in Japanese, he says, "I am just winding down with my evening rounds, Sweetheart. I will be home soon."

He listens to a female voice on the other end of the line and then replies, "Don't worry, I will. What? Yes, I will stop at the market on the way. Sure, it's getting late. Go ahead and put the children to bed."

Dr. Watanabe pauses for a moment and listens carefully. From the hallway, he hears the very dim sounds of beating Taiko drums. He hurriedly moves toward the door and peers out, first up one side of the hall, and then the other.

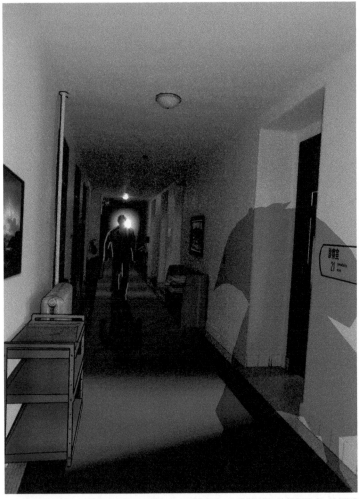

THE WARD ATTENDANT PAUSES AS HE PEERS INTO THE DARKNESS AND TRIES TO FOCUS ON THE LIVING SHADOW

"Hmm," he grunts. "Wonder what the beating drums are?"

The doctor goes back to his office, lifts his briefcase, turns out the lights, and walks out. In one corner of the office, a patch of shadows moves, shadows that weren't there before. The darkness parts and a set of steely eyes peers from the gloom. They are the eyes of Tenkai-Bo.

Jun sleeps restlessly in her room, turning one-way and then another. The faint beatings of drums interrupt her nighttime thoughts, for in the twilight of sleep there exists the nondescript arena of dreams between deep slumber and wakefulness. Jun's eyes open briefly to the haunting sounds of Taiko drums only to close again. The drums beat louder. In her sleep, Jun feels the tall figure of a strange man take her arm. And then a pinch, like the thrust of a needle. The sounds of the drum fade away along with the sinister shadow, since everything for her merges once more into a land of dreams and illusion.

In the hospital parking lot, Dr. Watanabe sits alone in a trance-like state in his car, staring toward the unknown. His world is now filled with the incessant melancholy beating of the ghostly drums.

"GOOD MORNING, SUNSHINE," Steve says opening the window-blinds in Jun's hospital room. "Rise and shine and greet the world 'Hello!'"

Light floods the room and causes Jun to stir in her bed. When she sees Steve, she tries to sit up but can't; she's confused.

"What? What is it? What are you doing here and why so early?"

"Early?" replies Steve. "Early – it's nearly ten o'clock."

"Can't be," blurts Jun. "It . . ." and then she sees the wall clock that reads five-past-ten. "For crying out loud, I should already be up." Jun attempts to rise but then falls back onto the bed.

"You okay?" asks Steve, suddenly concerned.

"I'm fine. Just a little dizzy."

Steve laughs, "That's what you get for sleeping late and trying to sit up so quickly."

"You may be right. Umm, my bones ache and my stomach hurts."

"I'll get the nurse for you," volunteers Steve.

"No, never mind. You're probably right. I just overslept. Besides, I want to get out of here.

"Yeah! Daiki told us you would be released today," says Steve, placing his hand on her forehead. "You don't seem to have a fever. You've probably been in bed too long. Anyway, I thought I would come over to get you. Daiki's busy."

Steve's last statement hurts Jun who recalls that Daiki had promised that he would pick her up.

"Jun, I just want you to know, that I always am thinking of you."

Steve leans over and tries to kiss her, but she pulls away slightly.

"What is it?" he asks. "I don't understand. I thought that we…"

Jun lowers her head in deep reflection and then straightens up, looking directly into Steve's eyes.

"Steve, I'm sorry. I really am. There is no easy way to say this, but I don't want to lead you on. There is no 'we.'"

Steve is stunned, and for a moment can't say anything. With his eyes narrowing, he blurts, "Is it Daiki?"

"I am so sorry, Steve. You are a wonderful man, but it could never be the same between us. Yes, it is Daiki. He and I have always had some kind of connection. I've known that for a long time, but don't ask me to explain it because I can't."

A knock at the door interrupts the conversation and breaks the awkward moment.

"Come in," yells Jun.

"Hi, there!" greets Daiki walking in and is surprised to see that Steve is there, too. "I thought you were returning to the library?"

"You told me that Jun would be released today, so I stopped by to offer her a ride."

Daiki nods but then adds, "I told her earlier that I would come by to . . ."

There's another surprising knock at the door. Dr. Watanabe peeks around the corner and then comes in.

"Good morning, Doctor," greets Jun who turns to Steve and says, "Good thing you woke me up."

"You met Daiki last night, Doctor," says Jun.

"Mr. Ike, right?" asks Dr. Watanabe.

"Yes," replies Daiki bowing, "You've got good memory."

"Ike is an unusual name; easy to remember, though."

"And this is my friend, Steve Chan," adds Jun.

Chan bows slightly.

"Mr. Chan," says Watanabe, returning the bow.

The doctor walks to the end of Jun's bed and takes her medical charts. Daiki stands to one side and away from the bed. Steve, feeling rather awkward after having heard Jun declare moments ago her feelings for Daiki, walks behind Dr. Watanabe.

Dr. Watanabe's demeanor abruptly changes and he becomes very serious. Walking close to Jun, who has moved to the side of the bed, he says, "Miss Lee, there is something, uh, very important, that I must discuss with you."

Jun is taken aback by the seriousness of the tone.

"In private, if you please," insists the doctor.

"Please, Dr. Watanabe, anything that you say, you may say in front of Daiki," she declares.

Steve, already hurt, winces slightly at being excluded. Jun notices this and adds, "And my friend, Steve."

Steve has his back toward them, but rotates slightly in Jun's direction to hear what's going to be said.

"Very well, Miss Lee. When we examined you after you were admitted, I discovered that your red blood cell count was very low. You were weak and injured, so I attributed the symptoms to the nature of your accident and perhaps an increase in the white cells."

"What is wrong with her," asks Daiki.

"Her red blood cell count has remained low which has caused a decrease in the production of functional leukocytes, the white blood cells.

We took a blood sample during the night and discovered that her condition--your condition--Miss Lee, has worsened. I suspect that you must be feeling weaker this morning, am I, right?"

"Yes, a little. My stomach hurts and I'm having some difficulty breathing," says Jun.

Becoming alarmed, Daiki asks, "What exactly are you saying, Doctor?"

"I am afraid, Mr. Ike, that Miss Lee is in an advanced stage of myelogenous leukemia."

Daiki freezes at the doctor's revelation. In shock, Jun lowers her head to avoid meeting the eyes around her. Steve turns sadly away.

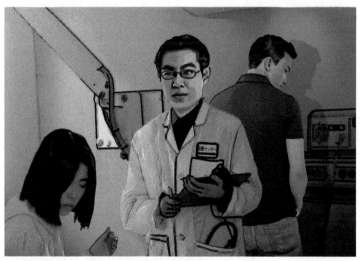

"I AM AFRAID, MR. IKE, THAT MISS LEE IS IN AN ADVANCED STAGE OF MYELOGENOUS LEUKEMIA."

DAIKI STANDS, SAD AND REFLECTIVE IN THE
MORNING HOURS, WITH ONE FOOT AGAINST THE
WALL OF HIS GRANDFATHER'S TEMPLE. JUN WAS
DYING AND HE WAS FEELING GUILTY.

LEGACY
Chapter Fifteen

STEVE CHAN SITS BY himself on one side of the room at the inn. Daiki stands close by, but is clearly lost in thought. Their collective expressions, moreover, are doom and gloom. Others are trying to cheer them up.

"They do wonders in medicine these days," says William.

"That's for certain," chimes in Jose.

"I'm sure Jun will recover," adds Violet.

Steve lowers his head as he slams his fist on the table, causing the computer screens to vibrate.

"There is no cure for myelogenous leukemia," he cries. "Jun's disease is one where the bone marrow produces too many white blood cells. It affects all the other red blood cells, white blood cells as well, and platelets. In the end, she dies." William and Violet turn to Daiki. For a moment Daiki remains speechless.

"Steve is right," says Daiki as he regains his composure. "Dr. Watanabe says that Jun's leukemia is in the late stages, that her spleen is critically enlarged, and the amount of blast cells in her blood and bone marrow will soon overwhelm her system."

"What are you telling us then?" asks Violet.

"That there isn't any cure for myelogenous cancer," replies Daiki. "I can't get an answer from her doctor as to when they will start any kind of treatment, so I don't know what's going on. It's very frustrating." He drops into a chair once more and then lowers his head. "My endless regret is that I never told her. I never told her, and it's too late now."

"Told her what?" asks William.

"That I love her."

Everyone is surprised. They know that Jun likes Daiki, but they don't know that he feels the same way toward her. With a pained look on his face, Steve glances over at Daiki.

"You can tell her now," coaxes Violet.

"I can't," says Daiki. "How would it sound and look? She's diagnosed with cancer, and I wait until just now to say it to her."

"Why didn't you say something earlier," says Steve, with a note of anger in his voice. "You know how she feels about you, don't you? Of course, you do!"

"I do," exhorts Daiki, "but I have so much on my plate with school, work, training, and all that."

"What you're saying is that they are all more important than she is!" contends Steve.

"No, that's not what I'm saying. It's just that, it's . . ."

"That is exactly what you are saying," counters Steve.

Daiki doesn't feel angry because there is nothing much he can say. His heart is filled with grief and guilt with the knowledge that he has made a very serious mistake in his judgment of the recent events.

"Hey, lay off him, Steve," barks William. "That's enough!"

"William's right!" exclaims Jose. "Enough, already." Daiki walks toward the door.

"No, Steve's right. I should have told Jun. I should have come over here with her when she asked me to. This is on me, guys."

As Daiki leaves, Violet angrily turns on Steve. "Now, there! See, what you've done!"

THE MIDMORNING LIGHT GLISTENS through the trees of Grandfather Daichi's sanctuary where Daiki has gone to be alone . . . to be alone, to think, to reflect. He stands up, sad and reflective in the morning hours, with one foot against the wall of his grandfather's temple. Jun is dying and he feels all the guiltier about it.

"This place is even more rundown in the daylight hours," mutters Daiki. Boards that had once been painted bright red are now dull and bare. The roof is in dire need of repair; and the shrubbery, that used to be cultivated with care, now spreads across the grounds like an unkempt carpet. Yet, this is Daiki's home . . . the only place left for him . . . the only place he knows.

"You are not going to listen to me, are you?" comes a soft whispered voice, seemingly out of nowhere.

Daiki, startled, looks around but sees no one.

"Nor, are you going to follow what I tell you, even when they are for your own good," continues the whispering voice.

Daiki looks to one side and then another. There is no one in sight. Thinking he hears something behind him, he spins quickly only to face emptiness.

"I am here," says the voice directly behind Daiki.

Again, Daiki spins around, and this time finds himself literally face to face with his grandfather.

Daiki is confounded and at a loss for words, but the grandfather continues emphatically, "We cannot stand here in the open. Come, let us move inside where we can talk and listen to each other better."

The exterior, now overgrown with broken and ripped rice shades, blocks much of the sunlight that once brightened the temple's interior, but the grandfather makes no move to open them. The light that comes in penetrates only through dated holes and tears in the wall.

Daiki and his grandfather skip the living quarters, but instead take positions opposite each other on tatami straw mats. Broken beams of light stream dimly through the kato-mado, a temple window shaped like a lotus flower. A single candle on the floor nearby furnishes the only direct illumination of the room. Somehow, Daiki feels that the flickering candle shines more on him than on his grandfather. Nonetheless, Daiki decides to confide in his grandfather, to tell him of his sorrows since leaving Japan; to tell him of the conflict he feels at disobeying his grandfather's instructions; and the unbearable loss and shame he feels for not helping a man who early on has saved his life.

The grandfather displays little emotion, but listens quietly as Daiki relates his story. Finally, he speaks of his enormous guilt and grief for the way he has treated Jun. Daiki realizes that some of what he is relating to this grandfather he already has discussed with him, but he feels it important that they are brought up again and put new light into them as well in the context of events presently occurring.

When Daiki speaks of the mysterious apparitions and visions he has had while in Los Angeles, and the mystery surrounding Kukai's scroll, his grandfather's eyes glimmer and his focus intensifies. For a moment, Daiki feels that his grandfather sympathizes with him when he speaks of Jun and his love for her. Daiki sees something his eyes have never seen before. Tears are welling up in his grandfather's eyes!

"Nothing is going right," says Daiki. "I know the puzzle is a clue left by Kukai, but I cannot figure it out. There is nothing I can do to make things right with Dr. Thompson. And now, with things the way they are, how can I tell Jun that I love her? She may think I am saying it out of pity toward her."

Daiki leans to one side and asks, "Grandfather, you are my only family and I mean no disrespect, but these problems are very real to me and I desperately need your guidance . . . your help.

"We have not trained together for many years, young man. Let us do so, now," replies Daichi.

Daiki stands.

THE GRANDFATHER LISTENED QUIETLY AS DAIKI SPOKE OF THE GRIEF AND GUILT HE FELT FOR THE WAY HE HAD TREATED JUN AND DR. THOMPSON.

As Daiki rises, he observes a single candleholder placed on the floor adjacent to his grandfather. Like his yo-yo, it too has the familiar Yin-Yang symbol. "Perhaps, it has always been here, I can't remember," thought Daiki.

Both men step into the large training area.

"Here, you may change," says Daichi, tossing his grandson a Keiko-Gi, a martial arts training uniform. "It is old, but clean."

Daiki changes quickly and then moves to stand opposite his grandfather.

"Let us see, what you remember," says Daichi.

Both men bow and then take their respective martial arts stance. Suddenly, without warning, the grandfather advances on the younger man, knocking him aside with an abrupt forearm blow. Daiki quickly recovers his balance and manages to block two blows, one from a fist and the other a single kick. Each quietly circles the other when once more, Daichi shifts to the grandson's left, to strike a blow. Daiki moves to block it but the blow never comes because the grandfather repositions to Daiki's right side, instead. Daichi repeats the identical maneuvers four times, first shifting to the right and to the left. Daiki successfully blocks each movement.

Daichi backs away four steps and circles Daiki once more. This time Daiki is prepared. Daichi rushes forward with a speed and agility that one his age should not possess. First, he advances to Daiki's right as before. As Daiki raises his arm to block the advance, Daichi repeats the familiar shift to the left. This time Daiki sensing this would happen literally beats his grandfather to the punch. Instead of blocking as he has, he raises his forearm to eye level as a protection, but delivers a hard punch to Daichi's midsection. The only problem is that the grandfather is not there to receive the punch.

Daichi had only feigned a move to the left, but had remained on the right. This movement left Daiki's entire side unprotected. The grandfather takes advantage of the moment and delivers such a sound kick to Daiki's shoulder, that the grandson slams to the floor.

Caught completely unaware, Daiki hits, then slides along the floor mats. The grandfather drops his martial arts pose, approaches the grandson and stands over him.

"Water flows here and flows there. It may appear to flow on and on, never changing, always seeming to be the same, much as a gentle river. We observe this and become accustomed to its flow. It makes us see its movement even if there is none, because we expect to see it. Our adversaries, like the flow of water, can change and make little alterations that we do not see because we do not expect to see them. These are like the very real currents that lie under the water. In time, a river may widen itself from erosion or carve out new tributaries for it's current. The water above and the water below does the work. We do not see or suspect the water below. The flow of water teaches us that our adversaries can do the same."

Daichi says nothing more, waiting to see if his grandson understands the lesson.

THE GRANDFATHER MOVES WITH A SPEED AND AGILITY THAT ONE HIS AGE SHOULD NOT POSSESS.

Daiki lifts himself from the floor and facing his grandfather, says, "In other words, we train our selves to see what is continually before us and if it changes or is no longer there, we see not what it is, but what it was; what we expected it to be."

"Exactly," smiles the Grandfather. "What we expect to see, we see. There is more to a flow of water than what is before our eyes. As a current continues in its course, it carries with it the air above it and the fish beneath. It eats away at the banks, erodes and changes the landscape."

"None of which we see if we do not expect it," interjects Daiki.

"Correct," rejoins Daichi. "Depending upon what the flow of water does, the air above it may change as may the fish below it. The air may heat or cool, the fish may grow larger or smaller, diminish or multiply."

Daiki nods his head, understanding what his grandfather is saying, "So if I believe something to be true, I will see it as true even if it is not. In short, what I expect to see, I see. What I expect to believe, I believe. Therefore my eyes will see it even though it is not there."

"Unless you train to see what is not," counters the grandfather.

"How do I do that?"

"By expecting the unusual – those things that may not be, but which could be," declares the grandfather, smiling and backing away toward a dark corner of the room into which he suddenly vanishes.

"Gone again," mumbles Daiki, who searches the empty shadows but finds nothing.

An echo of the Grandfather's voice reverberates throughout the training room, "Like the flow of water, young Daiki, expect the unexpected, suspect the normal and remember, there may not be any dragons in front of you or behind you . . . but there might be. Therefore, expect to see them!"

Daiki stands alone in the room questioning whether the Grandfather was going to help or had he already helped him. What to make of his grandparent's discussion of water, dragons, and the unexpected, he didn't know.

One event in the encounter with the Grandfather stood out in Daiki's mind. His Grandfather had not lectured him on the necessity of leaving. That was important. He had also offered him advice in his own way. That was important as well.

Daiki removed his martial arts uniform, folding it neatly and removing his blue shirt from the pile of clothes he had stacked earlier. As he did so, his eye caught something he had not seen before. It was a book . . . a very old book, almost falling apart from age.

As he lifts the book, a large sheaf of papers drops from a folder affixed to the back cover. Daiki quickly picks them up from the floor and reorders them in sequence.

"Poetry," he thought. "Wow, this is all hand written." Then he notices a handwritten notation at the top of the page:

> *English Translation*
> *of Kobo Daishi Poetry*
> *by Daichi Ike*

"This is my Grandfather's writing. He's translated something by Kobo Daishi."

"Kobo, Daishi," mumbled Daiki. "Wait, Kobo Daishi is the honorific name given to Kukai."

He reexamines the original book written in old Japanese lettering and then checks the lettering against the English.

"Holy smoke," exclaims Daiki in a loud voice, "I'm holding an original ancient book of poetry, written by Kukai and an English translation of it by my Grandfather!"

IT WAS A BOOK...A VERY OLD BOOK, ALMOST FALLING APART FROM AGE.

THE DEVIL'S PLAYGROUND
Chapter Sixteen

I T'S BEAUTIFUL, DAIKI," DECLARES Jun, carefully holding the frail antique book of Kukai's, "Your Grandfather left this for you and translated it into English as well?"

"I think so, yes," replies Daiki.

"Listen to this," says Jun as she reads from the old volume. "That everything is impermanent is the way all things come into and go out of existence. It is when these processes are over that we see true happiness in Nirvana. What do you suppose Kukai means by this when he says all things are impermanent?"

"Impermanent," muses Daiki. "In and out of existence. Wonder if these are the things my grandfather has been talking to me about?"

"Maybe," replies Jun, "Your grandfather, like Kukai, is or was trying to tell you something, that's for sure. He cares for you, I can tell."

"Maybe, I don't know. Anyway, I need to get back to the inn to help William and the others. I'm dead certain that this book has some meaning, some hidden significance. Would you mind keeping it for me? Perhaps you can read it and see if you can find some clues hidden there. When we finish at the inn, I'll come back. It'll be later tonight."

"I'll look it over," Jun promises as Daiki walks toward the door. Daiki stops and turns back, and for a moment is seemingly altogether lost in thought.

"Yes?" asks Jun.

"I don't know how to . . . how to . . . say what I . . ."

Daiki walks back toward Jun's bed whereupon she takes his hand, looks directly at him and quietly says, "You want to say that you love me!"

Daiki, pleasantly surprised by her frank response, can only stammer one quick answer, "Yes!"

For the first time, the two hold each other . . . tenderly and closely . . . their lips meet in love's first kiss.

STEVE, WILLIAM, JOSE, VIOLET, and Daiki sit at the local Tsukasa restaurant that specializes in fish and noodle dishes. They are all despondent and obviously exhausted.

"Damn it all," blurts Steve. "This has to be a hoax. Kukai is playing games. There's no message to be had."

"You may be right," adds William. "Perhaps he never intended for anyone to solve this mathematical enigma."

Daiki, even more frustrated, slams his chopsticks on the table and burst out with, "Damn!"

"Damn, damn, damn! I need some air," screams Jose disgustedly. He stands, walks to the door, slides it open, and immediately jumps back, startled! Standing in front of him is Captain Sato.

The ever-smiling Capt. Sato brushes past Jose and draws near Daiki and the others. "Oh, me! What a gloomy bunch you are this evening. Are the noodles not to your liking?"

The five students look guilty of something, even though there's nothing for anyone of them to be guilty of.

THE FIVE STUDENTS LOOK GUILTY OF SOMETHING, EVEN THOUGH THERE'S NOTHING FOR ANYONE OF THEM TO BE GUILTY OF.

Capt. Sato continues. "All of you appear as though you haven't slept for days. Surely, your new expensive hotel rooms are not uncomfortable, are they?" He walks around the table, stopping at Violet's seat.

"Oh, but you must like your rooms. You seem to be spending a great deal of time in there."

A thought quickly passes through Daiki's mind.

"We're being watched. The local police are tailing us. But why? I don't understand this."

Daiki stands up and says, "Very nice to see you again, Capt. Sato. We are just leaving; but here, please take our table. We hope that you enjoy the noodles as much as we have."

Everyone immediately vacates the table and steps out of the diner, and leaves Capt. Sato behind standing alone once again and rather discomfited.

Outside, the students pile into Daiki's car. They are clammed up until William breaks the silence. "Forget about what I said about Kukai. There's something going on here. They wouldn't be tailing us if there isn't."

"You caught on to that, too, huh," says Steve. "Count me in. Let's go back to the inn."

"I agree," says Daiki. "There's another key to this puzzle, one that we don't have yet."

"Has to be!" exclaims Jose. "We just need to keep working at it until we find the solution."

"Trust me. We will find it," affirms Daiki. "We will find it!"

HUNDREDS OF YATA-HA MONKS, attired in Shugendo martial-arts uniforms, are training in an open, large, and torch-lit cavern. They exercise in pairs with each Shugenja wielding a six-foot staff as a weapon. The barefoot martial artists display a highly regimented demonstration of footwork as they engage one another in trial combat, weapon against weapon.

Sou Ki-Bo, Tenkai-Bo's chief lieutenant and Martial-Arts instructor and robed in a white raven Shugenja uniform, stands taller than all the rest. His keen eyes survey the exercises, eventually settling on two sets of monks who fail to meet his expectations.

"What are the four of you doing?" yells Sou Ki-Bo who immediately snatches a stick from one closest among the four Shugenjas. Facing the remaining training partner, the instructor challenges the monk to repeat the movement. As the monk, does so, the trainer strikes the opponent's staff with an upward sweeping movement and then in a sudden downward arc, knocks the man's legs from under him.

"It is this that you should be doing," quips Sou Ki-Bo when the opponent falls.

A hush suddenly passes over a horde of practicing Yata-ha as the tall and muscular figure of Tenkai-Bo bursts in the room. Unlike the others, he remains masked, his felt presence manifestly ominous.

"Continue!" orders Tenkai-Bo in an authoritatively loud voice.

Sou Ki-Bo raises his arm and the monks resume their training. Tenkai-Bo strolls through the practice lines, his dark-brown-almost-black eyes peering through his green raven's mask as he intensely studies and examines the Shugendo practice maneuvers. Then without warning, he averts his eyes to the same four trainees whom Sou Ki-Bo has just corrected.

"Stop!" yells Tenkai-Bo in a voice so commanding that all the others stop as well. He steps directly toward the four, and upon approaching them asks,

"Did not your trainer just correct you?"

The warriors lower their heads.

"This is not a ballet workshop for little girls. When you have a weapon, you do not wave it about like a majorette's baton. You use it as an extension of your own body."

Tenkai-Bo seizes the weapons from one of the monks, reaches for the end of the pole and pulls out a hidden double-edged metal tip from its end, which then clicks and locks into place. He throws the pointed staff back to the original holder with such force that it jolts the Shugenjas back several steps.

Never taking his eyes off the warrior-monk, Tenkai-Bo snatches the staff from the monk's former training partner and repeats the motion of drawing out and locking the metal tip. He turns to the remaining two and demands, "What is it you are waiting for?"

The two terrified Shugenjas immediately replace their weapon's ends, switching each to a two-sided spear. Tenkai-Bo, never breaking eye-contact with the first monk, orders Sou Ki-Bo to arm the fourth monk, which Sou does immediately.

No sooner has the fourth monk set his spear than Tenkai-Bo moves right into the center of the four monks so that two are standing in front of him and two in the back. Neither has he broken eye contact with the first monk.

"Now, attack me!" whispers Tenkai-Bo in an eerily gentle voice. "Attack me!"

All four Shugenjas are shaking, frozen out of fear. Tenkai-Bo's voice grows louder and gruffer as he commands, "Attack me!"

Finally, one of the monks, standing at the rear,

approaches Tenkai-Bo and thrusts his spear toward the face. Without breaking eye-contact with the first monk, Tenkai-Bo shifts his upper body to the left and then to the right, away from each of the spear thrusts.

Tenkai-Bo swings his weapon in alternate back-and-forth movements as he advances toward the monks to his front, forcing them backward. The two monks at the rear step forward, each trying to take advantage of the front monk's retreat. But Tenkai-Bo's actions are so accurate, precise, elegant even, that the monks cannot compete. As one of the Shugenjas drives his spear toward Tenkai-Bo, the demon warrior swings his weapon upward, blocking the opponent's downward thrust, and then makes a three-hundred-sixty-degree counter-motion that forces the monk's spear fly into the air. In the same quick movement, Tenkai-Bo cruelly slices the man's forearm.

The Shugendo spear flies into the ceiling and hangs there. The other two monks, now standing behind Tenkai-Bo, attack with the hope of taking him down. But Tenkai-Bo's power is obviously potent and overwhelming. He circles around the monks and faces them head on. In a single swirl of motion and using only his left hand-held weapon, Tenkai-Bo disarms the monks, whose spears fly across the floor. Next, Tenkai-Bo uses his instep to kick up into the air both spears that are on the floor, now flying toward the two warriors who are facing him. Each spear strikes the right legs of both monks, leaving them bleeding and in pain.

Tenkai-Bo then spins in place and mercilessly

slices one of the remaining two monks across the stomach. Although the wound isn't deep, it's painful and bloody nonetheless.

The fourth monk shakes terribly in fear and begins striking wildly at Tenkai-Bo's face, but the demonic fiend easily blocks them all, and without hesitation lacerates the monk's arms in several places. Four helpless monks are down and bleeding, but Tenkai-Bo's gaze stays fixed on the first monk, as it has been right at the beginning of the surprised battle.

"What are you all waiting for? Get up!"

The monks reluctantly lift their weapons. While doing so, Tenkai-Bo executes a startling one-hundred-eighty-degree turn; spins and lashes out at the monks, this time penetrating whatever is left of their defense, and relentlessly and ruthlessly slicing their forearms, shoulders, legs, and stomach.

The entire training room is hushed in fear and in awe of the spear-wielding devil. The downright cruelty and stark hideousness is not lost on any of them. But they, too, are just as evil and heinous. It reckons then everything is in its proper order.

The offending monk, with whom Tenkai-Bo has maintained constant eye contact the entire time since he came in, is now in dreadful fear such that he breaks away and runs ferociously toward the cavern's opening, seeking to escape.

Tenkai-Bo's unremitting, cold-blooded eyes never flicker. His heartless, unfeeling expression remains as is when he lifts a spear from the floor and heaves it high into the air, at the same time twirling his two-sided weapon toward the flying missile-like spear and strikes it mid-air, hurtling it toward the monk with whom the Tenkai-Bo has never broken eye-contact.

The flying spear cuts the side of the monk's face, after which Tenkai-Bo sticks it into a heavy wooden training post directly behind the fallen monk. The cavernous room is deathly quiet and mute as terror, fear, and dreadful awe compete for space.

Tenkai-Bo walks between the bloody disciples who lie on the ground holding their wounds and trying to suppress their cries of pain, lest they be forced to fight again.

"You see," mockingly says Tenkai-Bo in a strained, modulated voice that nonetheless reverberates throughout the room, "No pain, No gain."

The masked, devil-figure Tenkai-Bo then turns to Sou Ki-Bo and whispers, "Today, I have put into motion events that will adversely impact our young American visitors. Come with me. There is more that I would have you do. This will require two of your men. I have chosen Tsubame and Taka."

The chamber of monks clears a pathway for Tenkai-Bo's exit, and follows three steps behind Sou Ki-Bo. As they pass, the crowd subconsciously steps backward to avoid the devil's wrath. Behind them, however, is the offending monk who groans with agonizing pain from his wounds inflicted by Tenkai-Bo.

THE FLYING SPEAR CUTS THE SIDE OF THE MONK'S FACE BEFORE LODGING INTO A HEAVY WOODEN TRAINING POST.

Tenkai-Bo stops and raises his hand. Immediately two masked Yata-ha guards emerge from the darkness and carry the whining monk away into another patch of endless black obscurity.

As the two Yata-ha guards fade into the black darkness themselves, the hollowed sounds of a high-pitched scream echo throughout the chamber . . . a stony-hearted chamber that is truly and literally the devil's playground.

DAIKI SPRINGS FROM THE LANDING, STRIKING THE FLEEING INTRUDER.

THE LISTENERS!
Chapter Seventeen

WILLIAM CARRYING A HUGE stack of papers, anxiously paces the floor. He crosses to the wall, glances back and forth between the pages of calculations he totes and those on the wall.

"Nonsense," he mutters. "This is all nonsense. It's meaningless."

The printer shoots out additional sheets which William snatches and then repeats his analysis. "Aaaarrrrrrrg!" he screams. "Nothing again."

William's other friends, busy at their workstations, pause at the outburst. They turn for a minute, look at him and saying nothing, merely return to their work.

"I mean, come on guys, tell me again why we are doing this?" demands William.

"For treasure," quips Violet.

"A fortune," adds Steve.

"Right. Yeah. Okay, thanks for reminding me," replies William.

A clicking sound at the door interrupts the group's laughter. As they turn to face the door, Daiki enters.

"What?" he asks, surprised that everyone is staring at him.

"It's nothing," says Steve. "We're all nervous, what with Captain Sato lurking around."

"I understand. I don't know what he wants, other than for us to leave Japan. It seems the sooner, the better for him."

"That much is obvious," interjects William.

"To say the least," mumbles Jose.

"Anything yet?" asks Daiki.

"Nothing," replies William. "I ran every single calculation that you gave me plus another dozen of my own and still, all the computer spits out is garbage."

"Garbage in and . . . " interjects Violet.

"Don't even say it," warns William.

"No, wait a minute," cautions Daiki. "I think she's right."

"What do you mean," asks William. "We're entering the numbers just as they are in Kukai's riddle, right?

"Yeah."

"And, we've looked systematically at every possible arrangement of those numbers, correct?"

"Okay," says William. "I take it that you are going somewhere with this? "Kukai's smart, but no one can beat out the calculations a computer can do."

"That's what I mean, William," replies Daiki. There must be another key to the puzzle. And, we don't have it."

"Have what?" asks Jose.

"The key that unlocks the riddle."

"Well, duh!" states William.

"No, no, follow me on this. What do the facts tell us so far?"

"I dunno," retorts William, "You tell me."

"They tell us that we haven't found the underlying key, the key necessary to unlock whatever information Kukai was concealing. You see William, you're right. They didn't have computers back then so Kukai had to have something, something that made all of his other numbers make sense. That is exactly what's hidden from us, now."

Outside the door, a shadowy figure slither's along the hallway, stopping only when it has reached the door to Daiki's room. It leans close, listening quietly, unmoving. The voices coming from inside the room can be faintly heard and Taka is listening.

"So if what you say is true, then what's the key?" asks Violet.

"That, I don't know," replies Daiki despondently. "It's somewhere in all of this but I can't find it."

Steve steps forward, "Maybe we should . . ." His conversation is interrupted by Daiki's cell phone.

"It's Jun," says Daiki as he answers the device. "Yeah, Jun, what's up?"

"I think I may have found the key that you're looking for," says the voice over the phone.

"What?" exclaims Daiki!

"Maybe 'found the key' is too strong. But, I think I know what it may be."

Taka leans as close to the door as he can but in doing so places too much weight against it.

The students are surprised when the door pushes slightly ajar.

"There's someone outside," cries Violet.

"He's been listening," shouts Jose.

Taka quickly pulls the door shut and races along the hallway toward the stairs.

Steve is the first to exit followed by Jose.

"There he goes," yells Jose.

"After him," barks Steve taking off down the hall in pursuit.

Inside the room, Daiki explains the situation to Jun; "We can't talk about this over the phone. But we'll be at the hospital ASAP. Hang on." He pockets the cell phone and rushes through the doorway.

"They've gone after him," yells Violet, "at the end of the hall!"

Daiki sees Steve and Jose chasing after a dark figure racing toward the stairwell. "William, stay with Violet and watch the room," orders Daiki. "I'm going after them."

Steve and Jose round the corner leading to the stairway landing, when suddenly the hall lights snap off.

"Aiiiii!" shouts Steve slamming into the back of Jose.

The only light in the hall comes from a small window at the opposite end of the hall but where they stand, the darkness is all-pervasive.

Daiki heard Steve's cry and runs even faster. Suddenly, he hears another noise, a shuffling sound – and it's somewhere near his friends.

Daiki squints through the darkness searching for something, anything. Running closer, he sees it, not in front of where Steve and Jose are looking, but emerging from a darkened alcove behind them. It's the faint shape of someone clutching a long rod. A rod or tube, several feet in length is pointed in their direction. Yet, it is too faint for him to make out exactly what it is. Then he observes that the rod is no longer aimed at his friend, it's aimed at him. Instinctively, the young Japanese swerves to one side as he hears a dull thud of something striking the wall near where he had been. As Daiki continues forward, he sees the long wand like apparatus no longer veering toward him, but back in the direction of his friends. The device and shape have moved into the hall light and Daiki can better see the object.

"Get down," screams Daiki, "Hit the floor."

Steve and Jose, confused with the loss of light, coupled with their friend's cries, nonetheless drop to the floor. As they fall, the hissing sound like that of a flying wasp is heard as the mysterious weapon spews out a needle shaped object.

"It's a blowgun—stay down, "shouts Daiki again.

Everything seems to spin in slow motion for Daiki as he sees the weapon's deadly dart whizzing in his friends' direction.

Jose releases a loud painful cry as he falls forward against Steve.

A second hissing noise sounds through the hallways, as a second dart-like needle buries into the wall adjacent to where Daiki is passing. He dives for the floor but then immediately stands and races toward his friends.

The attacker crosses the hall and from the sound of footsteps on the stairwell, Daiki knows that the shooter is escaping. He reaches the stairs, spots the figure near the bottom step and springs headlong toward the shape flips through the air and slams hard into the escaping villain, and sends him sprawling into the Inn's small lobby area.

THE HISSING SOUND LIKE THAT OF A FLYING WASP IS HEARD AS THE MYSTERIOUS WEAPON SPEWS OUT A NEEDLE SHAPED OBJECT.

Daiki releases his grip as he falls and somersaults over the gunman, landing on his feet. The rouge quickly twists, aims his weapon at Daiki and fires. However, the young boy is no longer there, instead he has advanced to one side of the would-be killer, kicking the weapon from his hand. Taka attempts to stand but as he does so, Daiki moves forward, preparing to engage him. However, he is struck from behind and slumps to the floor. Stepping from behind him is Tsubame, another sour-faced henchman of Tenkai-Bo.

"We should kill him," exclaims Taka as he retrieves his weapon from the floor.

"No. That was not our order. We leave now!"

"Waiiii," cries the Innkeeper, stepping to the counter from his small office to investigate the noise.

Tsubame immediately snatches the weapon from his goon's hand and fires one of the deadly darts point blank at the Innkeeper who collapses behind the reception desk.

Daiki struggles to stand up as the two henchmen escape through the front entrance. When Daiki hears groans from behind the counter, he promptly investigates and finds the innkeeper unconscious still alive but unconscious. Daiki checks the innkeeper's pulse rate, grabs the hotel phone, and then calls for an ambulance. A wild scream is heard when the innkeeper's wife walks in and sees her husband lying on his own pool of blood behind the counter.

"His pulse is okay, but he is unconscious. I've called for an ambulance and they'll be here shortly," explains Daiki while carefully removing the dart from the innkeeper's shoulder, and making sure he does not touch its tip.

"This may be useful. The police must be notified about this," Daiki thinks as he slips the dart into one of the inn's envelopes he finds lying on the counter.

"There may be another victim upstairs," Daiki notifies the wife as he hurries from the inn's lobby area and swiftly climbs the stairs, two and three steps at a time. He rounds the corner and sees Steve holding Jose.

"Daiki," bowls Steve. "Jose's been hit. I think he's dead."

DAIKI SCURRIES DOWN THE hospital hallway until he reaches the intensive-care nursing station. He goes directly to the head nurse and is about to ask her when he hears Violet's sobs from around the bend in the corridor.

"Never mind," he addresses the nurse, and runs toward where the sobbing sounds are. He finds William standing outside the door to one of the intensive care unit consoling Violet."

"How is Jose? Is he...?" inquires Daiki.

"No, he's not dead. He's okay," replies William. Daiki dashes into the room but William cautions him "You can't go in there. The doctors are with him now."

"Then how do you know he's okay?" asks Daiki.

"It's some kind of poison that they can't identify yet, but they say he should be fine," says Violet.

"They also say Jose's vital signs are unaffected," adds William. "The innkeeper is doing well also. He's right down the hall still unconscious."

"Does Jun know about this?"

"Yes. She was here until Dr. Watanabe found her and asked her to go back to her room."

"Are you all right, Violet?" asks Daiki. She nods that she is. "William, please stay with her. I'll be back shortly. Before all this happened, Jun says she has something important to tell me. It may have something to do with what's happened."

"I've got everything under control here, pal. You go ahead," urges William.

Daiki leaves the two behind and hurries toward Jun's room in an adjacent hospital wing. He knocks on her door and barges in.

"Daiki!" exclaims Jun. "I just heard. Jose, is he..."

"He's going to be fine. The doctors are with him now."

Jun takes Daiki's hand and pulls him up close.

"What's happening?" asks Jun in bewilderment. "First, Dr. Thompson and Michael are killed. Now, you, Steve, and Jose are shot at by some madman with a...a...what? Blowgun? And poor Jose is actually wounded. Something is wrong, dreadfully wrong!"

"I agree. This much is obvious: something or someone doesn't want us around here. I saw the attacker at the inn. He had a direct bead on me. The odd thing was he didn't shoot, but instead turned his fire on Steve and Jose. He fired a second shot at me but I think he was just trying to distract me. None of this makes sense."

"William said you were knocked out?"

"Stunned, anyway. I never saw the second man, just the one eavesdropping at our door. When I stopped him, the dude from behind and whom I didn't see hit me. It didn't knock me out, but it did slow me down, enough for them to get away."

"What's behind all of this?"

"What and who are the questions," says Daiki looking away in deep thought. "Kukai's treasure spells and represents an untold fortune. No doubt others know about this."

"But how could they have found out about it? We're the only ones supposed to know. Maybe, Dr. Thompson expected this, but he's dead and, for sure, he didn't tell anyone."

"I can't answer that," says Daiki. "It's a real puzzler. If no one outside of our group knows then . . ." Daiki abruptly stops talking. A look of concern passes across his face. "No, there's one other and only one other person who knows."

"Who's that?" begs an alarmed Jun.

"My grandfather. I told him!"

"Well, that can't be," says Jun confidently. "He's your family."

"He's been acting strange since I returned. He didn't want to see me and has repeatedly asked that I leave. He appears and disappears without explanation. No, he's up to something. I can feel it in my bones."

"I would like to think that you're wrong," insists Jun

"I'm not," says Daiki firmly.

"Where is he staying?"

"That's another thing. I don't know. His home at the temple is deserted, in shambles, in fact. I don't know where he lives and he doesn't care to tell me. Still, whenever I want to see him, he's always at the temple."

"Watching you?" asks Jun.

"I think so. Maybe lurking is a better word. I'm going there now."

"Wait," says Jun. "Before you go, there's something I want to tell you. I may have found something, something important."

"Oh, yes!" exclaims Daiki. "It's one of the reasons I'm here." Then catching himself, rephrases his sentence, "It's not the only reason I'm here," then pausing again, and continues. "Certainly not the main reason I'm here."

"Here, take this with you," says Jun smiling as she hands him the antique Kukai book of poetry. "Read it later, but I have marked his Iroha."

"The Iroha Uta?" asks Daiki.

"Yes!"

"It's his most famous poem."

"I know," says Jun, "and it was famous during his lifetime. What I found interesting in studying the poem was that Kukai didn't use his usual combination of Chinese characters and Japanese letters in the poem.

"As he did with the puzzle," catches Daiki.

"That's right. He only uses the Kana letters."

"Traditional Japanese lettering?"

"That's right!"

"So, you think he's telling us something?" asks Daiki.

"Could be. When you have time, check it out. It may be a key."

"It may be the key. I hope so. I'll let you know what happens at my grandfather's temple."

Jun holds Daiki's hand tighter. "You must be careful. We're dealing with forces that we don't know much less understand. Even worse, they are forces that are trying to kill you . . . us."

"I know. I'll be careful. I'll check on Jose before I go, and then have William bring you up to speed."

"Be careful," Jun cautions.

"I will," affirms Daiki.

"Come back to me," she enjoins in a serious but loving tone that touches Daiki to the core.

Daiki pauses, looks at Jun, and gently, lovingly replies, "I will!" He then turns around, walks away, and heads toward the ICU.

Steve and Violet are outside Jose's door when they see Daiki heading toward them.

"He's all right," says Steve. "There's no damage other than a bad headache. The doctor says he'll be groggy for a while, but other than that, he's okay. Right now, he's out like a light."

"How are you doing, Violet? What can I get for you?" asks Daiki.

"I'm fine, I'm fine, at least now that Jose is okay. You're weren't hurt?" Violet asks.

"Fortunately, no!" says Daiki turning back to Steve. "Did you see anything back there?"

"I didn't see anything. Someone turned out the lights and then I heard you yell. When Jose was hit by whatever it was, he fell against me. I saw you go by me and then it seemed like someone else went by."

"Seemed like?" interrupts Daiki.

"Yes, very strange, because I can't say I saw someone; it's more like I felt a presence pass by and over me," recounts Steve.

"The light panel is located in the small alcove adjacent to the stairs," says Daiki. "A second man was waiting there. He's the one who turned off the lights.

"Was he the shooter?"

"I don't think so. I heard him giving orders to the first guy, so he must be the one with the blowgun."

"Who still uses a blowgun?" penetrates Steve. "Those are relics from the old Tarzan movies."

"Yeah, well, blowguns are relics that were used in Japan long before Edgar Rice Burroughs wrote his ape-man novels," clarifies Daiki.

"Any idea who these attackers are?"

"None. I'm as surprised as all of you."

William opens the door and steps into the room. "Okay, enough of this excitement. What now?"

"I'm driving over to my grandfather's temple."

"What's he got to do with this?" asks Steve.

"I'll tell you about it on the way over, if you want to come with me."

"Yes, sure," replies Steve.

"William, are you okay staying here and watching after Violet, Jose, and Jun? I'm afraid to leave them alone."

"I can do that, don't worry."

"We'll be back in a few hours. You've got your cell phone?"

"Yep."

"Good! I'll call you on the way back, and we can plan where to meet up."

"Got yah!"

"Let's go," says Daiki to Steve.

The three friends step out of the room into the hallway and directly into the presence of Capt. Sato. This time the captain isn't smiling. Not at all!

Capt. Sato says nothing but stares without a blink at the trio. After a long uncomfortable pause, he takes a long sip of tea from a cup that he's holding.

"So, let me get this straight. You, young men, claim you were shot by a blowgun-carrying Ninja?" says Capt. Sato quizzically.

"We never said anything about any Ninjas," blurts Steve.

The three young men are stunned at the turn of events, although Daiki is thinking that they shouldn't be. If Sato was suspicious of them before, he is certainly warier of them now, particularly after the twin shootings that they are unable to explain.

"Are you going somewhere?" asks Sato. "No, please be so kind as to let me rephrase that. Is there somewhere that you think you are going?"

THE THREE FRIENDS STEP FROM THE ROOM INTO THE HALLWAY AND IMMEDIATELY INTO THE PRESENCE OF CAPTAIN SATO. THIS TIME HE ISN'T SMILING. NOT AT ALL!

Taking another sip of tea, Capt. Sato adds. "Because I assure you, young men, that you are not. As of now, you may consider yourselves under arrest!"

THE EVIL TENKAI-BO

CAGE OF DEATH
Chapter Eighteen

TENKAI-BO STEPS INTO A small grotto off a much larger cavern. In the middle of the hollow are two of his men, Taka and Tsubame, both of whom are visibly anxious because of the impending entrance of their heartless leader any given moment.

The wicked devil of a leader says nothing when he strides in with all his arrogance. He seems to glide though. Tenkai-Bo is tall and lean and his cat-like movements add dread to the two men as he circles around them numerous times like a ferocious lion would its prey. He stops within inches of their faces, stares directly at them, and gives the impression that he's reading their minds. Taka and Tsubame are certain it is what Tenkai-Bo is exactly doing; and the mere thought makes them even more apprehensible.

Tenkai-Bo ambulates to the center--between his minions--stretches his hands outward, and holds them parallel to the ground for minutes on end. The arms neither tremble nor move as much as a breath when, abruptly, both hands shoot upward, hold up for a moment, and then slowly drop to his side. As the long, massive arms move down, a brand-new sound—faint, distant, and pounding--penetrates the hallways, rooms, and crevices of the enormous cavern. Some unknowing ones may ask what the sound is all about, or where it is coming from, but Taka and Tsubame very well know. They have heard it several times before.

The volume and tempo of the pounding and pulsating beats of the drum increases throughout the entire span of the cave, and the harmonies of terror float ceaselessly until they fill to the brim the heads of the henchmen whose mounting fear of their devilish leader escalates to the point of sheer desperation and panic.

The satanic-like Tenkai-Bo lifts his hand, a signal for the guards standing behind Taka and Tsubame to shove the two fearful men forward and who both then stop, once again, within inches of Tenkai-Bo. As usual, the repugnant leader's eyes are ablaze like burning coals in the mines. He peers without a blink into the minions' eyes, now brimming with unbridled terror.

For a moment, the tension is broken when Sou Ki-Bo shows up in the small, cave-like room. He walks close to his master, and with quivering lips very softly murmurs to him, apparently almost soundlessly. Tenkai-Bo seems to hear and understand, regardless.

The devil-fiend leans toward the two cowering figures before him and indignantly says, "You were given a simple task . . . to just listen and gather information. Instead, you have chosen to engage the enemy and used weapons that have, up to now, alerted the authorities." Again, the demonic Tenkai-Bo circles his prey, speaking angrily as he goes around.

"You did understand that I do not want our presence known until it is time, but you deliberately disobeyed me," says he and gruffly stops in front of Tsubame.

"Master, I could see no other alternative. The young one had knocked Taka to the ground; he was in danger of being caught."

Tenkai-Bo shakes off his confrontational stance and steps away from Tsubame to face Taka this time. Tsubame quietly sighs with relief, although he is still quite uncertain as to what will happen to him. He continues through with the rest of his personal narration.

"I could not risk leaving Taka for detention, so I did what I thought I should do then. . . Oh, merciful one!"

Tsubame slowly lowers his head, in part out of respect but largely to avoid Tenkai-Bo's incisive eyes the colors of which have just altered from a piercing brown to a smoldering cat-like green.

Taka is fully of aware of the change in Tenkai-Bo's eye-color. He faces a specter doing something that he has never witnessed before; and as afraid as he was earlier, his fear multiplied four-fold with the eye color transformation. Tenkai-Bo's horrid countenance now fully confronts the fear-stricken Taka.

The eerie throbbing of the drums continues, only much louder this time. Taka's shivering has considerably multiplied, and he cannot control even the slightest tremor. As his obvious fear mounts greatly he starts to collapse, but Sou Ki-Bo has a grip on him and holds him up more tightly.

Tenkai-Bo redirects his attention toward Tsubame. "I commend you on your actions. It is not the way I would have preferred to handle this, but it seems easier for you to tell me why you did something rather than why you did not."

Tsubame is visibly relieved, but no sooner has he exhaled than Sou-Ki-Bo has seized him with his other arm and propels him forcefully backwards.

Now it is Tenkai-Bo and Taka who stand toe-to-toe.

Tenkai-Bo raises his arm that immediately prompts the three Yata-ha Shugenja to march in. Two of them grab Taka, secure him firmly, and replace the former guards who hold him. Completely terrified, Taka feels he is about to collapse, but with two Yata-ha restraining him he just cannot. All that he can do is watch the proceedings through his sweat-drenched brow. Although drops of oily and salty perspiration painfully pour into his eyes, he stares ahead and dare not move nor wipe it away.

A third Yata-ha joins a fourth one who comes out from a slide-opening in the cave wall. Together they push a long coffin-like box to one end of the dark cave. The fourth guard opens the twin lids on the sarcophagus, showing sets of chain manacles at the top, center, and lower parts of the ghastly container. At the lower end of the box is a square hole that leads to the outside of the container. What that is for, Taka cannot guess; but he'll know the spectral answer to his question in the next few seconds.

From the other sides of the rock walls come screams like the cries of thousands of children in ominous danger and fighting for their lives.

A sliding door opens, and a fifth Yata-Ha with a large object in tow appears from the dark shadows.

The fifth warrior carries a cage of high-pitched squealing, gnawing, rats; each worked into such a frenzy that any one of them will fiercely and relentlessly turn on the other, unrelenting until its opponent lies dead.

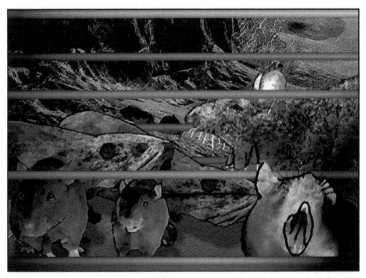

HUGE SCREAMING, GNAWING RATS, EACH WORKED INTO SUCH A FRENZY THAT ANY ONE OF THEM WILL FIERCELY TURN ON THE OTHER, UNRELENTING UNTIL ITS OPPONENT LIES DEAD.

The cage of ear-splitting, high-pitched rodents is solidly attached to the bottom of the longer box. Taka can see that the only thing that prevents the devouring scavengers from entering the lower portion of the box is a small sliding door that separates those in the metal cage from the wooden crypt.

Tenkai-Bo says nothing but nods his head, a signal for the two Yata-ha to drag Taka to the dreadful apparatus. Frightened to the core, Taka can't even manage a scream. The only thing he can do is emit a pitiful, fearful squeal matched only by the infernal terror in his eyes.

"You have failed, Taka," intones the devil. "Failed, when we could not afford to. There is a penalty for all Yata-ha Shugenjas who disappoint me."

Tenkai-Bo holds out his hand and waits for the fifth Yata-ha to place a chunk of bloody raw meat into his palm.

Taka's eyes widen with unmistaken horror, even more so now than earlier, when he sees his raven-masked, demonic leader dump the meat through the metal bars at the top of the cage to the restless, squeaking rodents inside.

Instantly, the screeching vermin rip the meat just as the other rats tear at it in their race to devour the bloody morsels that have been tossed into their habitat.

Tenkai-Bo's pale green eyes glow with extreme satisfaction, while the drums beat louder. Taka's head turns back-and-forth from the gnawing rats to the green eyes that match the wearer's green mask. Taka is definitely lost as to which of the two he is more afraid.

The raven-masked Tenkai-Bo nods once more, whereupon Taka is immediately raised into the air and instantaneously deposited into the box where his feet and waist are securely manacled. The lower door is closed and his neck is shackled to each side of the wooden casket-like tomb of terror.

Taka's eyes grow wider while he continually squeals and watches Tenkai-Bo cross toward the small sliding door at the end of the container where Taka is.

"There are three gates," says Tenkai-Bo. "My pets must pass from one to the other, gnaw their way through to their final destination. They are starving and will not stop until the food is gone, until there's no more to chew on." The monstrous Tenkai-Bo briefly pauses and then continues his wrathful tirade. "It will hurt at the first gate. But, oh, not nearly as much as the second. There's enough pain for a man to faint because of shock but, don't worry, Taka, that will not happen to you."

Tenkai-Bo glances toward Sou Ki-Bo who immediately releases a small metal box from his belt-container. He settles the box down on the coffin lid and opens it to reveal a small glass medical syringe with a long needle. Tenkai-Bo removes the syringe, tests its contents by squirting a tiny portion of the solution from the needle into the air. Then, without so much as a warning, he thrusts the needle into Taka's neck where the whole sticky contents empty into his bloodstream.

"You need not worry about fainting now," continues Tenkai-Bo, "simply because the injection guarantees that you will remain awake when my carnivorous companions begin their feast. You will still be conscious and alert when they chew their way through the first chamber and then on to and through the second one. Your faculties will be diminished, of course, but you will be aware when they gnaw their way toward your brain."

The heartless monster of a raven says nothing more, but instantly removes the sliding door that separates the ravenous creatures from the first chamber where Taka's feet and legs have been lodged.

Taka's growing pathetic squeals turn immediately to full-throated agonizing screams while the rodents rush through the cage's opening and begin devouring the fresh meat that awaits them.

The first Yata-ha begins closing the lid, but is stopped by the malevolent raven-masked demon.

"Leave it. I want others to understand the penalty they have to pay for plain disobedience or failure to follow my instructions. Besides, I find that Taka's screams are rather pleasant to listen to."

Addressing Sou Ki-Bo, the demon further gives his orders. "Have three guards remain. The others may go."

Tenkai-Bo's eyes return to their natural dark-brown state. The sounds of the beating drums taper off until their volume is overpowered only by the continual screams of the manacled and hapless Taka.

Sou Ki-Bo withdraws with his master. They both leave by the entryway through which Taka's coffin has been produced. As the entryway closes, Tenkai-Bo turns toward the screaming Taka, and then mockingly quips to Sou Ki-Bo, "You see--waste not, want not."

The entryway slides shut, leaving only the three guards and a throng of excited vermin chomping at their quarry at the same time tearing through the thin wooden slides that separate several compartments of the sarcophagus.

FOR NOW, THERE IS LITTLE TAKA CAN DO BUT SCREAM AND WAIT.

The cavern chamber is soon empty, except for the three Yata-ha Shugenja sentries who remain at the gate. The sounds of beating drums subside and then vanish. Still, there linger unmistakable, persistent sounds: the macabre clawing, chewing, gnawing, gluttonous shrieking and yelping of the omnivorous rats as they feast their way through the first panel and tear away at the second. For Taka, however there is no death or cessation of pain just yet; there will be none until the furry flesh-eaters shall have gorged their way into the third chamber. For now, at this nauseous moments, there is little Taka can do but scream and wait.

THE YIN-YANG ODYSSEY!
Chapter Nineteen

"**Y**OU CANNOT CONTINUE to hold us, Captain. You absolutely have no grounds!" exclaims Daiki, sharply.

"You attack your innkeeper, Mr. Chiba, and then claim that some raven-masked creature did your work for you. Come on, now, do I look like a simpleton, or is it that you actually believe that we rural policemen are all fools?" replies Capt. Sato, as he suddenly changes his tone to irate indignation.

"The innkeeper is our witness to the attack. He's in the hospital, unconscious from getting himself hit by the blowgun," remarks Steve who gets angry at the captain's incessant questioning.

"And you expect me and this police department to believe that you were attacked by some Ninja dude with a blowgun?" answers Capt. Sato laughing. "You've been watching far too many movies."

"And I am telling you, Captain," Daiki adds, "that these two were real and their blowguns were real. You have one of their darts."

"Something that you no doubt lifted from one of the museums or temple archives you have been slipping off to," remarks the captain.

Daiki sighs and looks down, trying to recollect his thoughts when Capt. Sato's phone rings.

"Sato, here," answers the captain. "Yes, Lieutenant, what did you find out? Have you spoken to his physician? He's close? Good, talk with him, I'll hold." Capt. Sato lowers his phone to address Daiki and his friends. "I sent Lt. Asano and Sgt. Suzuki to the hospital to check out this wild tale of yours."

"Wild tale, Captain! You were there when the innkeeper was brought in," Violet throws in very irritatingly.

"Brought in because of your friends' attack. He was unconscious when they brought him into one of the wards."

"So was Jose," insists William.

"Unless you're saying we did to Jose what you claim we did to Mr. Chiba," blurts Daiki.

"Is that a confession, young man?" asked Sato.

"A confession?" Steve yells, beginning to lose his control. "A confession! Are you nuts? This is insane, certifiably insane, Captain. Totally!"

"Hold it, Lt. Asano is back. Unlike you, he will add clarity. Yes, Lieutenant, go ahead."

Steve glances at Daiki who shrugs his shoulders and glances at Violet who, in turn, shakes her head in disgust.

"What!" the captain shouts. "Are you sure of this? Positive? Make no mistake, understand me? Make no mistake!"

It's apparent from Capt. Sato's expression that he doesn't like what he hears. After several more minutes of conversation, apparently with Lieutenant Asano doing most of the talking, Capt. Sato slams the telephone into its cradle.

"It seems your friend is awake and he corroborates your story. Mr. Chiba, the innkeeper, is also awake and, like your friend, backs up your tall-tale."

"I told you," Daiki says, but before he can finish what he's about to say, Capt. Sato interrupts.

"I certainly find it too much of a coincidence that both of them have regained consciousness at nearly the same time."

"Well, duh, Captain!" says William exasperatingly. "They were shot at the same time."

"I don't believe in coincidences," says Capt. Sato, repeating his oft-heard phrase.

The police detective's eyes narrow as though he's deep in thought and then says, "The doctors confirm there was a poison in their system. It's a very ancient poison, one not seen for more than a hundred years."

"What is it?" asks Daiki.

"Shuku-cha, or so the doctors said. None of them has any idea where it came from. Hell, none of them could say how it was made."

"Then, you have no grounds to continue to hold us and you definitely cannot arrest us," presses Steve.

"You may go but don't leave the district just yet. Something about all of this doesn't feel right," warns Capt. Sato. "Your friend is at the hospital, waiting to be picked up."

The group starts to leave.

"You may pick up your stuff at the front desk," says Capt. Sato. "Mr. Ike, would you please stay behind for a few minutes?"

Daiki lingers while the others file out the door. "Yes, Captain?" he responds inquiringly.

"I was a young man when your parents were killed. I had just started on the force at that time and, along with my partner, was assigned to the case, more specifically to investigate your grandfather's conspiracy theories."

"Conspiracy about . . . ?" Daiki challenges.

"Your parents' death," immediately says the captain. "None of his theories ever checked out, but in the process of our investigation, we found plenty to be more suspicious of him than of any other individual or circumstances."

Daiki listens attentively and carefully and says nothing so as to let the police captain to continue, and he does.

"So, you will forgive me if I don't find your stories of secret conspiracies plausible," says the captain.

"But you heard about those who attacked us, the men in black-bird masks," Daiki fills in.

"Oh, yes! Black outfits and raven masks, I believe you said."

"Yes, and Mr. Chiba said so, as well," confirms Daiki.

"Ah, yes, Mr. Chiba. A simple man who has lived his life never having been attacked so that when something like this happens his imagination gets overblown."

"Imagination!"

"Indeed, Mr. Ike. First of all, your attackers were burglars, no doubt about it, thieves who were pilfering the guest rooms when you spotted one of them."

"And the blowguns?"

"Nothing. The hospital said that the poison on the darts was negligble, perhaps even diluted. It could never have killed you. I am sure these cheap rate thugs used it in self-defense. Not many guns in Japan like you have in America. They couldn't get them so they used these harmless toys."

"And the masks, the black suits?" penetrates Daiki.

"Halloween costumes, nothing more."

"What!" Daiki exclaims in exasperation.

"It's all very simple and nothing more than a series of coincidences that you have used to support your wild theories."

Daiki walks to the door but before stepping out, he turns to face Captain Sato.

"You don't believe in coincidence, remember Captain?"

Sato sits up straight and gives Daiki a penetrating look.

"It may surprise you, sir, when I say, neither do I!" says Daiki finally, then turns around, and leaves.

THE FRIENDS GATHER AROUND Daiki in a semi-circle. "When we got back last night, I read and re-read the poem that Jun gave me."

"The Iroha Uta?" asks Steve.

"The same," replies Daiki. "I think Jun was on to something. I had assumed that Kukai's hidden riddle concealed in his star was all about random numbers. But when I read the poem, the one you see pasted to my left, I thought it might be part of the puzzle. It is not. It's part of the solution."

"You mean, it's the key," asks Jose.

"I believe so!" Daiki says.

"But how?" quizzes Steve.

"Here, let me show you," replies Daiki. "Remember, I said that the poem wasn't written in Kukai's usual combination of Chinese and Japanese letterings?"

"The Kana!" interjects Violet.

"Exactly. Kukai wrote the poem in Kana, and I'd like to think that he used it only to direct us to the puzzle's solution," says Daiki before he continues on.

"And here's a new chart that I made up early this morning," adds Daiki while he removes a large sheet of paper from the table.

"Obviously, you did this before we got up," Violet chimes in with smiles on her face.

"Take a look at how I've broken down the Iroha Uta poem, syllable by syllable." Daiki fastens his chart to the wall and then carries on.

"Notice that I have numbered, from one to forty-eight, each syllable that's here. Underneath each syllable is the Kana letter, and below it is its pronunciation to help us a bit. This, I truly believe, is the key."

"So, now what do we do?" asks Steve curiously.

Daiki thinks for a moment and then replies, "Only one thing left for us to do."

Kukai's Iroha Uta Broken Down Letter by Letter

Each Kana letter numbered in order of appearance ⟹

Using this chart we can decrypt Kukai's Star by analyzing all possible combination of numbers and letters around the "Star"!

1	2	3	4	5	6	7	8	9	10
い i	ろ ro	は ha	に ni	ほ ho	へ he	と to	ち chi	り ri	ぬ nu
11	12	13	14	15	16	17	18	19	20
る ru	を wo	わ wa	か ka	よ yo	た ta	れ re	そ so	つ tsu	ね ne
21	22	23	24	25	26	27	28	29	30
な na	ら ra	む mu	う u	ゐ wi	の no	お o	く ku	や ya	ま ma
31	32	33	34	35	36	37	38	39	40
け ke	ふ fu	こ ko	え e	て te	あ a	さ sa	き ki	ゆ yu	め me
41	42	43	44	45	46	47	48		
み mi	し shi	ゑ e	ひ hi	も mo	せ se	す su	ん n		

B.

"HERE'S A NEW CHART THAT I MADE UP EARLY THIS MORNING," SAYS DAIKI

"We must run every possible combination of random numbers and letters, until we come up with something. It's not like we have to start all over again; we've got this exercise down pat, for sure. Let's get back to work, shall we?"

DR. WATANABE WALKS INTO his office, pulls the window blinds, and then sits at his desk and leans back. He sighs, relaxes, and shuts his eyes to give them a little rest, only to be interrupted by a knock at the door.

"Come in," says Watanabe.

His office nurse enters.

"Yes, Ms. Funai, may I help you?"

"I'm just coming on duty. Is there anything you need, Doctor?"

"No, thank you. I'm resting a bit. I was on call last night and didn't get any sleep at all. I need this for a moment."

The nurse smiles understandably, then replies, "You go right ahead, Doctor. I'll see to it that no one disturbs you."

"Thank you," says the doctor. Ms. Funai closes the door behind her.

Hardly has the doctor closed his eyes when he hears a faint sound of beating drums. On this occasion, however, Dr. Watanabe doesn't look where the sound is coming from. Instead, he stares straight ahead as though in a trance. In his mind, he hears a hollow, whispery yet commanding voice. It is that of Tenkai-Bo.

"You did well, Dr. Watanabe, as I have commanded."

"I injected the girl the injection with the serum you gave me," replies the doctor.

"And her symptoms?"

"*Myelogenous* leukemia, as you said."

"And the cancer treatments?"

"Delayed as you ordered. However, I must start them just as soon if we are to..."

"No!" commands the voice. "You are not to start them. Delay them under some pretense!"

"I understand," says Dr. Watanabe.

"There is another task that I'd like you to do. It's an important one where the timing is vital. Here are my instructions. You must follow them explicitly," the authoritative voice says.

"I understand," the doctor replies. And the cavernous whisper fades away.

JOSE SCREAMS AT THE top of his voice, "AAARRRGGG, I give up. I quit. It's not working!"

"Calm down, it's working," says William. "Look, patterns are actually forming and are starting to make sense."

"None of this makes any sense to me," adds Steve.

"No, not yet," says Daiki, "But William is right. Patterns are forming, but we don't have the computing power to run them out."

"What are you saying?" asks Violet.

"We need a much bigger computer!"

Everyone in the room turns around and stares at Daiki in great disbelief.

"Which means?" asks Jose?

"Which means we need more computing power. We must contact someone who can get us access to a supercomputer."

All at once, everyone's stare rotates from Daiki to William.

"What? Why are you all looking at me?" is all that William can say with a bit of a surprise in his tone.

"Because you are the only one among us here with that access," says Steve. "You are our Mr. Harvard man!"

"Steve's right," adds Daiki. "You went to Harvard, William, and you're a computer guy. Do you know someone who can help hook us up there?"

"I did go to school with John Coulson. We're in all the programming courses together."

"What else?" Violet asks.

"He is the chief assistant at Harvard's computer center."

"Will Harvard's computer do the job; you think?" asks Violet.

"Do the job!" replies William. "Harvard University's supercomputing cluster called Odyssey boasts of a 14,000-core Intel Xeon architecture with over 10 TB of RAM. It can handle anything we want to do."

"Do your stuff then, William," says Daiki. "Get us hooked up to Odyssey."

Everyone cheers, encouraging William to make the vital call.

"John is on the other side of the world. He's probably asleep now."

"This is important. Wake him up."

"I'll see what I can do. This will take a while. Go on up to the dining room. I will join you later. If you hang around while I'm calling, it'll make me nervous."

Daiki smiles as he proceeds to usher everyone out of the room. William picks up the phone.

An hour later, when Steve, Daiki, Violet, and Jose are drinking coffee in the inn's dining area, William bursts into the room.

"We're in!" he shouts. "We're in."

"What does that mean, 'we're in'?" asks Violet.

"It means that Daiki's computer system is connected to Harvard's Odyssey. It can make 10.51 quadrillion calculations per second!" exclaims William excitedly.

"And John is waiting!"

Everyone cheers loudly.

"One catch, though," says William.

The cheers stop.

"We only have an hour's time on the computer. It's the best John can do and he's even scared to do that. You have any idea how much this is costing Harvard just for one hour?"

The others look perplexed thinking they may have to pay for it.

"Never mind, you don't want to know. Don't even ask; they're picking up the tab."

"For one hour?" asks Daiki"

"One hour, and that's all. So, whatever it is we have to do, we must do it now and do it quickly."

"HARVARD'S ODYSSEY CAN MAKE 10.51 QUADRILLION CALCULATIONS PER SECOND!" EXCLAIMS WILLIAM EXCITEDLY.

"Listen, guys. No one has solved Kukai's riddle for the last 1,200 years," reminds Daiki. "With the supercomputer, maybe we can do it in the limited hour Harvard has given us."

"Let's hope we all can," remark Steve, Jose, and William simultaneously.

"I'd say it's a good sign," Violet says with a chuckle. "When can I start?"

"Right away; right now! John and I have your computer logged into Odyssey. It's waiting for you."

Everyone jostles over one another as each scrambles for the exit.

A. Kukai's poem on the scroll must be translated and understood!

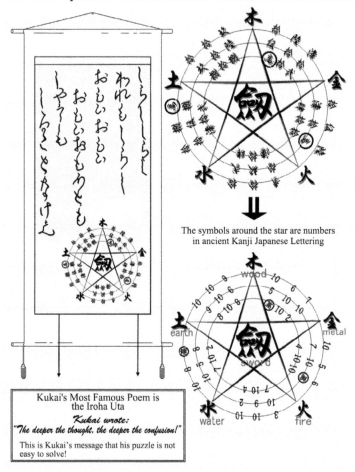

The symbols around the star are numbers in ancient Kanji Japanese Lettering

Kukai's Most Famous Poem is the Iroha Uta

Kukai wrote:
"The deeper the thought, the deeper the confusion!"

This is Kukai's message that his puzzle is not easy to solve!

"LOOK AT THE OLD CHART AGAIN. I'VE LABELED IT CHART 'A' OR STEP ONE."

CHASE!
Chapter Twenty

JUN STARES FROM HER window and watches a large Japanese Nissan police van pull into the hospital loading docks below her room in the hospital. She has not seen the vehicle before, but feels she should have, one way or the other.

"I have spent enough time standing at this window," reflects Jun. "But why just now? That vehicle looks more like a funeral hearse than a van."

The police van is solid black, not the customary white-and-black patrol car, and its windows are unusually darker.

"Can't see in. I wonder who it is in there!" Before Jun can think any further, four policemen and a clinic attendant in hospital-green gown step out of the vehicle.

"Hope they're not here for me. With this cancer of mine, I reckon one day they will be," she sighs.

Jun's leukemia diagnosis has been all too sudden for her. She has never experienced any symptoms of the disease, but since her stay at the hospital, she's been feeling continually weaker and weaker; and her body-aches don't seem to let up.

The door to the room opens and Jun swings around to see Dr. Watanabe coming in.

"Good afternoon, Miss Lee."

"Doctor," acknowledges Jun. "Is it time to start the treatment?"

"Soon!" the doctor replies "Very soon! But first, there are a few more tests that must be run. Will you please accompany me?"

"Sure. Is Ms. Funai coming?"

"No, she's off for the day. It's just me. I hope you don't mind?"

"Not at all," laughs Jun. "Let's go."

"It's a little cool in the halls and especially downstairs in the radiology department," says Dr. Watanabe. "We're going down the basement, so you may want to put on your robe."

"Good idea," replies Jun as she takes her robe from the closet and leaves with the doctor.

Jun and Dr. Watanabe take the elevator to the second floor several levels below her room. As soon as they reach the radiology department, she takes off her robe and with Dr. Watanabe's instruction settles herself on a long hard-black table. "I don't know where Ms. Honda is," the doctor says.

"Ms. Honda?" asks Jun.

"She runs this department and she is usually here. Well, it doesn't matter, really. I know how to do the barium."

"What is the barium and what is it for?"

"It's a simple test. We have you swallow barium . ."

"Which is?" interrupts Jun again.

"Barium is a white liquid that shows up on an x-ray. Once it's inside your body, the barium coats the lining of the stomach or intestine. Afterwards, it outlines certain of the body's organs on the x-ray. If there is a detected tumor from the cancer, it shows up as an irregular outline near the affected part of the body."

"I understand that, Doctor," says Jun in a rather surprised voice. "But, are you saying that I have tumors?"

"Sometimes one kind of cancer may manifest itself in other ways, such as tumors. Remember, your leukemia is in the advanced stage. Before we begin treatment, we want to check everything."

"I understand."

"Wait a minute, Miss Lee. Excuse me while I get the barium," says Dr. Watanabe. "I'll be back shortly."

Jun surveys the room as the doctor leaves. It seems odd to her that, except for the x-ray table, the room is remarkably empty. There isn't even an x-ray machine, neither is there the typical x-ray shield used to protect a technician while x-rays are being taken. The walls around her are blank; there are no x-ray viewers that usually are hanging on the walls.

Dr. Watanabe comes back in with a small glass of a milk-colored substance.

"This isn't tasty," says the doctor, "but you won't find it all that bad. Just drink it down quickly."

Jun swallows the liquid, after which Dr. Watanabe takes her by the shoulders and helps her lie down on her back on the long cold table.

"Now, just relax," he says soothingly. Then Jun begins to hear faint sounds of drums coming in from somewhere in the distance.

"You hear the drums?" she asks.

"Hear what?" responds Watanabe.

"Drums . . . beating drums," Jun says. Then suddenly a thought, a brief passing thought, flits through her mind. She has heard these sounds before. But where? And then she remembers.

"Professor Thompson's class," she cries.

"Who?" asks Dr. Watanabe.

Before Jun can say another word, she finds herself strangely getting groggy. She has trouble focusing and slowly feels that the large, flat x-ray table is no longer stable for her to rest on. She instinctively grasps the sides of the table to steady herself; but before long, she feels everything around her not stabilizing but swaying and spinning instead.

The drums beat louder, their sounds more intense.

"What is happening to me?" cries Jun, as the light in the room grows dimmer. Total darkness closes in and enfolds her while her breathing increasingly slows down. She tries to fight if off as she struggles to fill her lungs with air one last time before she finally collapses and her thoughts cease.

"WE'VE GOT IT, WE'VE got it," screams William at the top of his voice and continues to shout as he runs, jumps, and hops around the room.

The sudden, ear-splitting yell startles everyone in the room, as well as the few in the other rooms of the inn.

"Quiet down!" comes a shout from the room next door. Then they hear thumping on the floor beneath them.

"Whoa," orders Daiki. "We have neighbors now. Calm down. Shhhh!"

"But we did it. We did it," howls William in excitement.

"What's going on?" asks Steve.

"What's happening?" follows Violet.

Jose says nothing but waits for an answer.

"William is right," says Daiki, looking up from his computer for the first time in hours. "We've found something."

"What is it?" insists Steve.

"I'm re-doing an earlier chart to show you exactly what we've come up with. Just give me a few more minutes and I will put it up and explain it to you."

Steve, Violet, and Jose wait while Daiki works on a chart, which he soon tapes onto the wall, "This is our first step."

"First step?" asks Violet.

"Yeah. All of this is as simple as A, B, C, unless you read your ABC's any order you want. That's exactly what we tried to do, but we didn't see it until the supercomputer now gives us direction. Here, let me show you," Daiki says patiently.

"Our first chart should have been Chart 'A', but we treated it as Chart 'C'. That definitely didn't work out. Kukai's poem must be translated first and be understood later. We missed that, but thanks to Jun's reading of the poem she's able to bring it to our attention. Look again at the old chart which I've labeled Chart 'A,' or step one," Daiki continues with his explanation.

"We know that the symbols around the star are numbers, but numbers written in ancient Japanese Kanji. On this chart are letters translated in English, along with the other words right below them."

William steps forward and adds what he suddenly remembers.

"Kukai's statement, 'the deeper the thought, the deeper the confusion.' is his way of telling us this won't be easy to solve."

"And we almost didn't, at least until now," agrees Daiki. "Here is a second chart that I've made," and he hangs it next to Chart 'A'. Pointing to Chart 'B', Daiki moves on.

"Step two, or 'B,' is to number each Kana letter in Kukai's star in the order of each letter's appearance: from one to forty-eight."

"In other words," Steve interrupts, "the second thing is to break down Kukai's Iroha Uta by both numbers and letters."

"That is the 'B, Chart'" agrees William. "We have to analyze every possible combination of numbers and letters around Kukai's star."

"That's precisely the reason why we need a supercomputer; and we're able to get one, thanks to our William," proclaims Violet.

William stands and bows, his sandy hair spilling over and into his eyes and says with a smile, "Yep, thanks to me!"

Each Kana letter numbered in order of appearance ➝	Kukai's Iroha Uta Broken Down Letter by Letter									
	1	2	3	4	5	6	7	8	9	10
	い i	ろ ro	は ha	に ni	ほ ho	へ he	と to	ち chi	り ri	ぬ nu
Using this chart we can decrypt Kukai's Star by analyzing all possible combination of numbers and letters around the "Star"!	11	12	13	14	15	16	17	18	19	20
	る ru	を wo	わ wa	か ka	よ yo	た ta	れ re	そ so	つ tsu	ね ne
	21	22	23	24	25	26	27	28	29	30
	な na	ら ra	む mu	う u	ゐ wi	の no	お o	く ku	や ya	ま ma
	31	32	33	34	35	36	37	38	39	40
	け ke	ふ fu	こ ko	え e	て te	あ a	さ sa	き ki	ゆ yu	め me
	41	42	43	44	45	46	47	48		B.
	み mi	し shi	ゑ e	ひ hi	も mo	せ se	す su	ん n		

"THAT IS THE 'B CHART,'" AGREES WILLIAM.

Violet, looking at both William and Daiki, laughs and cajoles, "Okay, you two. You've got your supercomputer . . ."

"Thanks to me," William interrupts again.

The others join Violet in laughter.

"Yes, William," she says. "We all appreciate your help along with Harvard. We wouldn't have been able to get the computer without you, and with no funds either to run it . . ."

"For a full hour," adds William. "No charge!" Once again the room is filled with uncontrollable laughter.

"Now, take a look here at the good part," hurriedly quips Daiki just as soon as the laughter subsides, and lifts up Chart C.

"Daiki, you put any more computer charts up on the wall and you'll tear the wall down," warns Steve.

William steps back to look at the room. Sure enough, except for one tiny bare space, printed and lettered charts, numbers, and calculations cover the entire wall. It's on that bare space that Daiki hangs the last chart.

C. **Computer reveals that of all possible patterns, only one has meaning in its message!**

Counter-Clockwise: 88, 27, 47, 10, 14, 20 (高)

88	27	47	10	14	20	(高)
↓	↓	↓	↓	↓	↓	↓
no match (stays 88)	O	SU	NU	KA	NE	no match (stays (高))
	↓	↓	↓	↓	↓	

88 OSUNU KANE (高)

Only the "88, 27, 10, 14, 20 (高) combination makes sense. As for the "88 & (高) " it is obvious that

"88" = Shikoku 88 Temples

"OSUNU KANE" = Ozunu Kane = Bell of Ozunu (its meaning translated to English)

(高) = a temple related to the character "高"

Therefore, we must assume there is something in the 88 temples of Shikoku and those some things are related to the "Bells of Ozunu."

However, all temples have bells so "Bell of Ozunu. must relate to the temples established by Ozunu.

"TAKE A LOOK AT THE GOOD PART," QUIPS DAIKI.

"Our final step, or 'C,' is to work out every possible pattern from the random numbers that we have. The supercomputer has demonstrated that out of all the possible patterns, only one has meaning. Going counter-clockwise around the star, however, we see the numbers 88, 27, 47, 10, 14, 20, and the 高, or 'kou'," explains Daiki. "See! The message that we come up with is a simple one: 88 Ozunu Kane 'kou' or 高."

"Ozunu!" blurts Jose. "We know him from Professor Thompson's class."

"Let me explain further," says Daiki. "Ozunu Kane translates as Bell of Ozunu. The symbol 高

has to be a temple or something related to that letter."

"That something," interjects William, "is *some thing* that's related to the 88 temples of Shikoku and the bells of Ozunu."

"Whoa!" says Steve curtly. "Eighty-eight temples?"

The enormity of the challenge before them slightly diminishes the group's enthusiasm.

"Let's focus now on the bells," says Daiki.

"All the temples have bells," reminds Violet.

"That's right," confirms William.

"But not all the temples were established by Ozunu," comments Steve.

"Hey, you're right, too," says Jose. "Only four of them are."

"I agree," says Daiki.

"Then what?" asks Steve.

"William," says Daiki, "Take this chart and run it up to Jun. Fill her in on what we've found and see if she can add anything else. Steve, Violet, and Jose, you guys get ready to do some mountain-hiking."

"Where are you going?" asks Steve, a little perplexed.

"I'm calling on my grandfather to see if he can offer some clarity to all of this."

"Haven't you been through this exercise before? I thought you said you couldn't find him?" says Steve.

"I can't. But he always finds me. I'm heading over to his place to let him do just that. It may not do any good at the moment, but it's worth a try, particularly if he can offer a shortcut to the solution of our problem."

DAIKI WAITS IN HIS car outside his grandfather's temple for over an hour. No one has come or gone, which indicates no one has ever been there for quite some time. Uncertain, Daiki steps out of his car and walks toward the front entrance. Finding it locked, he goes around and checks every window as well as the rear entrance; still there's no way to get inside. Peering through each glass window, he can tell that the temple has been deserted, and run down, since the last time he was there. With no success in sight, Daiki lowers his head and walks toward his car.

A slight gloom overtakes Daiki who stands by his car for another fifteen minutes, his eyes trying to scour the woods for any movement, for any signs of life. Finding none, he opens and hops in his rented car. He sits there for a few minutes. Convinced that no one will show up at all, he turns the engine on, and checks his rear- and side- view mirrors to make sure no one is standing by. Seeing no one, he slips the gear in reverse and starts to back up. Careful that he is and for him to see better, he slips his arm over the back seat and turns his head to get a better view of where he is going. While doing so, whom does Daiki see but his grandfather sitting forward in the backseat and whose face directly positioned toward his.

"Ayieeeeee," screams Daiki, fully shocked and alarmed and surprised. "Cheesh! Crap!" he further exclaims.

"Say nothing but continue backing up," says Grandfather Daichi. "Check around you. What do you see?"

Daiki does as he's been told, but sees nothing. When he looks behind at the back seat again, no one is there anymore. The backseat is empty, vacant. He places his foot on the brake to stop.

"Go on. Continue. Don't stop!" comes the now-phantom-like voice of his grandfather. "You are being watched and you'll soon be followed. Do not leave by the temple road; take instead the one through the cemetery."

Daiki hesitates, but then hears his grandfather's voice again.

"You are in grave danger. Continue driving as though you suspect nothing."

Daiki is utterly shaken, but drives and leaves by the cemetery road as he's been told. Once outside the temple area, he turns onto the main road and drives away. A few minutes later, he hears his grandfather's instruction.

"Check behind you."

Daiki does just that, and then sees a brown-and-blue Nissan following in the distance. As he continues to watch the car behind him, Daiki occasionally speeds up and then slows down. The Nissan behind him does exactly the same thing--keeping pace and distance as Daiki does. At the spur of the moment, Daiki pulls his car to the side of the road and stops; the Nissan car behind him also pulls to the side of the road and stops

"For sure, I'm being followed," says Daiki in a very concerned voice.

"Yes," says the grandfather.

Peering in his rear-view mirror, Daiki is astonished to see his grandfather in the backseat.

"I do not want to be seen," says Grandfather Daichi. "Now it is imperative that we escape from them."

Daiki restarts his engine and slowly pulls forward. From the rear-view mirror he can see the Nissan car following him does the same.

"Follow my directions," orders the grandfather.

"I think I will follow mine," says Daiki as he stomps on the accelerator and causes the car to leap forward. Immediately, the Nissan car also speeds up. To confuse the car behind him, Daiki drives his car forward on the road and suddenly jerks hard on the wheel, which makes the car cross the opposite lane and on to a dense stretch of woods. Because of the force of the swift turns, the grandfather is thrown first to one side of the car and then to the other.

"Please, fasten your seatbelt, Grandfather," pleads Daiki who abruptly turns his car to the right, barely passing through a thick line of trees along the road that leads away from the woods. The trailing Nissan is not so fortunate; it made through the line trees but not without serious damage to the sides of the car.

Daiki reaches a long hill below which is a farmhouse in the distance. He floors down the gas once more and the car leaps over the hill and flies some twenty feet in the air before it lands roughly on a downward slope. Behind them is the roar of the trailing Nissan, quickly catching up and bearing down on its own. It, too, flies over the embankment, and Daiki knows it's only a matter of minutes before he and his grandfather are trapped.

Taken!

TAKEN!
Chapter Twenty-One

THE CAR PURSUING DAIKI and his grandfather flies into the air and then toward them. Daiki, afraid the trailing Nissan may land on theirs, shoves his rented Honda into a lower gear and pulls up his emergency break. The rented little car slows down slightly, enough to let the trailing car flying overhead pass them by.

Grandfather Daichi's seatbelt keeps him from rolling side to side, but fails to prevent him from bumping his head on the ceiling while the car hits the ground. A streak of expletives fly from his mouth as fast as the two speeding cars.

Daiki sees a second embankment and without giving it much thought instantaneously takes his hand off the brake, moves his car into high gear, and then presses the accelerator down to the very floor.

The trailing Nissan lands quite hard on the dirt, and seeing Daiki behind him, the driver tries to turn the Nissan unto the Honda. Unperturbed, Daiki drives directly toward the Nissan, terrifying its passengers such that their language begins to match that of Daiki's grandfather's a while back

When it looks like the Honda will strike the Nissan side-on, Daiki turns his car around and speeds up toward the second embankment. Aware of what Daiki is attempting to do, the Nissan driver decides to replicate Daiki's maneuvering.

Again, the little Honda flies over the embankment some thirty feet before landing, and continues its downhill slide, this time directly toward a farmhouse that looms ahead.

The pursuing Nissan again tries to duplicate what Daiki has just done, but it lands on only two of its side wheels instead of four, which causes the car to flip entirely over, land on its wheels, and then spin twice across the slippery grass until it regains its position and direction.

The Nissan is a larger car than Daiki's and is quickly gaining on him. Daiki never lets up on the accelerator and continues to speed down the hill toward the farmhouse. Regardless, the Nissan by all accounts is still a much bigger and faster vehicle and is now drawing closer and closer to Daiki's Honda.

Daiki gently pulls up on the emergency brake that gradually slows the small Honda and allows the Nissan to narrow the gap between him and the looming farmhouse. Just as if Daiki's car is about to slam into the house, he instantaneously yanks hard on his emergency brake and spins his wheel sharply to the right. The combination of a sudden break and the sharp turn forces the Honda to swerve about ninety degrees. As his car comes out of the rapid turn, Daiki releases the brake while he steps on the accelerator. The little Honda unbelievably shoots forward.

The trailing Nissan doesn't do as well. Its driver has been following the Honda too closely; consequently, he is not able to anticipate what Daiki will do next. When Daiki swiftly veers, the Nissan driver is unable to do the same; instead his car slips into a thirty-degree sliding incline and runs straight toward the farmhouse. The Nissan hits the farmhouse at an unalterable angle and thus buries part of its front-end into the building.

The Nissan attempts to back out and away from the smashed wall and broken boards of the farmhouse, but is forced to do so slowly, so that each move tears and rips at the car's finish. Only after numerous attempts is the driver able to begin driving away only to discover that a pitchfork-carrying Japanese farmer emerges from his house screaming at the top of his voice. When his eyes see that the vehicle that has just damaged his house is now attempting to flee, he flings his pitchfork headlong toward the escaping car. The Nissan flees the scene but carries along with it the farmer's pitchfork lodged behind the trunk of the speeding car.

Daiki is way well ahead of the chasing Nissan, and eventually finds his way back to the main road and proceeds to the next town. Looking in his rearview mirror, he feels a little relieved that no one's following him now. He turns his head halfway back to check how his grandfather is doing in the backseat.

With a vice-like grip, Grandfather Daichi is silently clutching his seatbelt, his eyes a bit wider than Daiki remembers of them. Feeling his grandson's eyes on him, Grandfather Daichi can only scoff at Daiki.

"Yes, I think that will do. We have lost them." Then a long silence ensues as the car rumbles on far into the distance.

Meanwhile, the Nissan's passengers desperately resume their search for the car they've been chasing. In sheer disappointment, Kiji, one of its passengers, orders the car's drive to stop. The Nissan pulls to one side of the two-lane rural road as Kiji reaches for his cellphone and places a call.

"We have lost them," says Kiji who listens more keenly to the voice at the other end. The conversation is more or less one-sided when a bleary but stern voice is heard coming out of Kiji's phone, to which Kiji loses no time replying.

"No, I did not see his face, only the young man's. Yes, I'm certain there is another man in the car, but I can hardly make of who it is."

The other three men in the car can only hear an unintelligible and very angry voice.

"I understand. We will continue to search," is all that Kiji is able to add.

The unmistakable sound of a disconnected phone heightens the tension felt by the other passengers in the car. No one dare says anything, least of all the scouring Kiji who cholerically urges the driver to move on. As the car pulls away, its right wheel wobbles from the damage it has sustained in the farmhouse: dents and gashes line the body of this once new and shiny Nissan.

In the village, Daiki pulls his car into a narrow side- street and stops. Neither he nor his grandfather has said anything since the chase. But now, Daiki has mustered to break the silence.

"Grandfather, you know I have Kukai's scroll." Grandfather Daichi quietly nods.

"And you also do know that it's a puzzle the solution to which leads the way to great treasure." The grandfather nods once more, but says nothing nor shows any reaction. Daiki, however, can tell from his grandfather's steely silence that he knows more than his countenance is telling.

"And since you do know a great deal about all these, Grandfather, I must make my own deduction that there is something about the scroll, or this chasing events, that you know a great deal about, but don't want to share with me."

The grandfather appears conflicted as though he wants to say something, but still decides to hold back.

"Since I've been here in Japan, in my country, in my home, you have been showing up and disappearing with no explanation of any kind. You speak to me of things you say I cannot understand, yet you expect me to leave the country immediately with no further questions asked, and all based on this bewildering unknown something or other."

"There is little I can say," replies the grandfather at last. "All I have done is spend most of my life trying to keep you from harm's way."

"Yes, yes, yes, yes, yes, Grandfather! You keep saying the same thing over and over again, but you don't understand I have no clue, much less an idea, what you have been talking about. The fact, Grandfather, is this. What you say in the absence of any evidence is all but meaningless to me. I'm totally at a loss!"

"You don't and cannot know how dangerous the scroll is; how dangerous the forces are, forces that have been set against you."

"Then, please, Grandfather, tell me that I may know so that I can do something, protect myself and my friends against those forces," says Daiki in an urgent, pleading tone.

Grandfather Daichi sighs, and momentarily glances down, seriously considering his grandson's request. A few seconds later, he raises up his head, turns around, and looks straight at Daiki's eyes.

"Many years ago . . . before you were born . . . there came a great . . ."

Daiki's cellphone rings, thus interrupting the grandfather. The grandson looks at his cell phone to see who the caller is. It's William.

"I'm sorry, Grandfather," says Daiki. "I must take this call. Please excuse me!" Daiki turns his head away and answers the phone.

"Yes, William!"

"Daiki, drop whatever you're doing now. Come to the hospital immediately."

"What? Why?" asks Daiki in a very apprehensive voice.

"Come quickly. It's about Jun."

"What about Jun?" Daiki is getting more concerned.

"She's been kidnapped," replies William.

"What? Is that true?" Daiki asks again.

"She is gone. She's been spirited away!"

"What about her doctor? What does Dr. Watanabe say?"

"He can't," responds William

"What do you mean, can't?"

"Dr. Watanabe is dead!"

Daiki is stunned. He turns toward his grandfather to tell him what has just happened, but the backseat is empty.

Grandfather Daichi is gone. He has left the car!

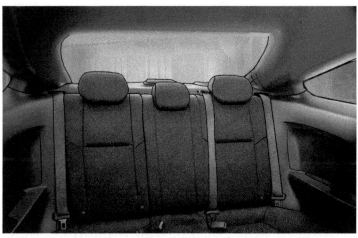

THE BACKSEAT IS EMPTY. GRANDFATHER DAICHI IS GONE. HE HAS LEFT THE CAR!

A voice that seems close, yet remote and far-flung, echoes within the car. It's a voice very familiar to Daiki, a voice he's been used to hearing every so often. It's unmistakably Grandfather Daichi's.

"Leaving Japan is no longer an option. I will come back for you. Do not forget what I have taught you, 'Unless you see what is not, you will miss much.'"

Daiki frantically checks over the car, but feels disappointed when he is unable to locate the source of a voice that he continues to hear.

"Expect the unusual – those things that may not be, but which could be. Whenever you quit chasing the things that are wrong, you give the things that are right, a chance to catch you."

A deafening silence soon follows, then comes one final piece of information.

"You are no longer alone!"

THE THREE FRIENDS EXIT the hospital and walk all the way to the parking lot. William tries to gather the group around him.

"Where's Daiki? Haven't seen him since he left," asks William, with Violet and Jose by his side.

"And Steve?"

"No idea," replies Jose.

"Upstairs with . . . no, wait a minute. Here he is," adds Violet who notices Steve coming straight toward them.

"Find out anything more, Steve?" inquires William.

"Nothing. Not a thing. They have no idea where they have brought Jun," says Steve sadly.

"And the doctor?" asks Violet.

"Dr. Watanabe has been murdered, that's all I know. The authorities found the body down in the basement in an x-ray storage room. The police are still there investigating," says Steve.

"You can bet, Capt. Sato will see to it that he has a word, or more, with us next," grumbles William.

"Sato wasn't there," says Steve, "I didn't see him."

"That's surprising!" exclaims Jose. "He's always 'Johnny on the spot' when it comes to trouble."

"Well, this time, no, he is not!" says Steve emphatically.

"How was Dr. Watanabe murdered?" asks Violet.

"Decapitated. His head slashed, cut off with some kind of blade."

Violet takes a deep, sharp breath, visibly disturbed by Steve's account of Dr. Watanabe's death.

"Why would anyone want to kill him?"

"Who knows," says Steve. "For that matter, who would want to abduct Jun?"

"Poor Jun," echoes Violet sadly and tearfully. "She's dying, and now mysteriously nowhere to be found!"

"Or why, we should ask?" says William.

Steve gives the parking lot a thorough look-over and blurts out, "Daiki's car is gone!"

"We know about that," says Jose. "We were talking about him when you were coming down."

"You think he's gone to look for Jun?" asks Violet.

"Perhaps. Yes, maybe!" replies William. "I don't know how he'll find her. He doesn't have any clue any more than we do."

"This isn't good. I don't like what's happening," says Jose after giving way to a long and heavy sigh.

In an out-of-the-way section of the hospital's parking lot, dark peering eyes sneak from behind a folded newspaper. It's Capt. Sato holding a telescopic listening device, and with the earpiece connected to it, studiously monitors the conversation of the young students.

As the friends walk away, Capt. Sato, with a tiny Machiavellian smile on his lips, lowers the newspaper a bit more and drops it on the seat beside him before he starts his car.

DAIKI SITS ON A ROCK above a cliff overlooking the ocean. He has driven to the Shikoku side of the cliff he remembers only too well when he was a very young child, and here hopes to collect his thoughts and be able to develop a plan of action he can readily execute. So far, he's been rather unsuccessful.

The sounds of the lapping waves below the cliff where Daiki is blend with the bass howl of winds sweeping the seascape. As well the gathering clouds taking on a heightening orange-and-yellow hue of an approaching sunset; and the pitch-black darkness of the sky helps obscure his thoughts. Jun has been kidnapped, his friends are in danger, and he himself has barely avoided a pernicious attack soon after his benign escape from a malevolent high-speed chase.

Daiki surveys the ocean and countryside that surround him with the grim thought that nothing has changed. But, he knows just as well that his thinking is absurd if not entirely wrong.

A lot has changed. Much of his entire life has been flipped upside down. His grandfather, the only family left to him, has been cold, distant, and elusive. Although Daiki feels certain that Grandfather Daichi can help him, his refusal to do so is obvious. To Daiki, his grandfather's sudden and mysterious appearances and quick disappearances have no purpose or reason at all.

All of Daiki's thoughts bring to the fore all circumstances behind his parents' unfathomable, mysterious deaths. Capt. Sato has alluded to some conspiracy theory allegedly attributed to his grandfather, but Daiki has never heard of it until then. Mr. Eric Sasaki, his guardian in America whom his grandfather has entrusted to raise him, has not made mention of it to him either.

Jun, the young woman Daiki has fallen in love with and dying of leukemia, has been abducted for no apparent reason. Her doctor has been found dead. Unseen forces have surrounded all the mystifying events. Indeed, they have kept continuous surveillance, followed and physically attacked him and his friends. Now they appear to be mounting a major offensive.

All the questions raised in Daiki's thoughts keep pointing to his childhood, one in which his parents were lost and when he had been driven from Japan. But why these and what about the strange visions he has had back at Mrs. Farmer's boarding house? And these weren't all the questions. There are many more!

The still-unsolved accidental death of Prof. Thompson and Michael Wood, Jun's abduction, and Dr. Watanabe's murder — are all linked to his parents' passing away. But how?

"What's the connection? Why are they linked together, and for what?" he wonders.

As if jolted from sleep, Daiki sits upright and shakes his head knowingly. The hidden treasure of Kukai--that must be it! Daiki allows himself a few moments to reflect on this and then says to himself, half out loud and in hushed tones.

"Whatever and whoever is behind all these seemingly fortuitous events, I will find and in the process, discover the truth."

Daiki has no plans as to how to solve his dilemma, but he's quite confident that he will soon come up with something. He will not leave Japan until he finds all the answers to the puzzle. This much Daiki is certain.

The young man sighs and lays his head in both his hands. The swells of the waves heighten and the low, dull sky is just about ready to embrace the evening hours. He hears in his mind Grandfather Daichi's voice that says he is no longer alone. At this moment in time, however, Daiki is but all alone! He is alone, very sad, and heavyhearted!

SOU KI-BO, THE CHIEF Shugenja lieutenant of the leader of the deadly Yata-Ha, stands in the middle of the darkness, in front of a static-charged electronic console. Before him are mounted a series of speakers with a large bank of microphones. Suddenly, the static is interrupted by a sharp hum. Sou Ki-Bo's hand moves over a light beam on the console's panel. The static stops.

"Speak," Sou Ki-Bo the henchman says harshly.

"We have taken all the documents from the Ike room at the Ryokan Inn," comes an oily voice over the speaker in the center.

"You have Kukai's records and papers?" demands Sou Ki-Bo.

"All of them," the voice replies.

"And the American work papers?"

"We have them as well."

"Bring them here."

"Yes, immediately

"Out," declares the henchman as he turns off the microphone which once again triggers the static noises.

Tenkai-Bo, tall and brooding, enters the epicenter of the small chamber that houses the Yata-Ha's communication center. His lieutenant steps to one side, giving way to the leader to take his position, front and center, before the console.

Seconds pass as Tenkai-Bo's keen eyes survey the dials. His gloved hand passes over a beam of light coming through between the control panel and the ceiling. Forthwith, the static ceases and the room becomes very quiet—so eerily quiet-- that the slightest move of the evil-master creates an exaggerated sound of fabric in motion.

Eventually the devil turns to face his chief Shugenja henchman.

"Report!"

"We have all of Kukai's documents."

"And the work papers?"

"All of them and our men relay that they have eyes on the young Americans."

"I am aware of that. Inform me of their surreptitious movements of any kind."

"I will. We tried to capture their young leader but he eluded us."

"I am aware of that, too!" said Tenkai-Bo. Don't concern yourself with him. He is within my control and I know exactly his whereabouts."

"What are your further instructions?"

"Bring the documents to me as soon they are in. If everything we need is there, then you will kill the others this evening while they're asleep. Do you understand?"

Sou Ki-Bo nods in agreement and then asks, "And you will take care of their leader, Daiki Ike?"

"Yes," says the demon leader who turns back toward the console that begins to irradiate when he passes his hand through the series of light-beams in the panel.

"Dismissed!" bellows Tenkai-Bo.

The devil's henchman bows low and backs through the entranceway, leaving his superior standing alone before the communication network.

The static in the room is replaced by a low hum. Tenkai-Bo then steps closer to the light-beam, his eyes focused on an increasingly brighter, pulsating light.

Tenkai-Bo's demonic eyes begin to change color, shifting from dark to light blue. The faint sound that surrounds the satanic-like figure reverberates, while the percussions grow increasingly loud until they get more pronounced. Slowly but steadily, the deafening drumbeats spread and fill every nook and cranny of the mammoth cavern.

They are the deadly drums of Tenkai-Bo!

TO BE CONTINUED IN:

**Follow Daiki's continuing exploits
as he unravels the mystery of Kukai's
treasure, struggles to save his friends and
rescue the woman he loves, but in the process,
incurs the treacherous wrath of Tenkai-Bo!**

About the Author, Warren Chaney

 **Warren Chaney** is an American author, filmmaker, artist, behavioral scientist, and pioneer in early television. He holds a Doctorate degree *(Behavioral Science & Management)*, an MBA *(Finance)*, and a Bachelor of Science with a double major *(Marketing & Speech and Theatre)*.

In a wide-ranging career, Dr. Chaney has written 25 books including 5 novels along with 16 screenplays, 9 theatrical dramas, and more than 250 professional and non-professional magazine and journal articles. He has written entries for *Colliers Encyclopedia* and was an editor for two publications, one in health care and the other, a fictional detective journal. He has produced 9 feature films and directed 8 in addition to producing and directing numerous television productions including 150 episodes of the pioneering television series, *Magic Mansion*. His work has received considerable recognition and numerous awards.

Dr. Chaney has a heavy background in behavioral science and management consulting and has been featured in national publications and mass media to include *Good Morning America, Real People, PM Magazine, CBS Weekend News and ABC Radio*.

Chaney established the first public university Health Services Administration program for the state of Texas, served on multiple boards of directors and advisory boards of public companies, and is considered a leader in the field of neuroplastic development of cognitive functions.

Chaney was an officer in the United States Army and served in multiple military commands during the Vietnam Era. He was born in Kentucky, a native of Hopkinsville, and was educated in Tennessee and Texas. Dr. Chaney now resides in Houston, Texas, is married and has five children.

About the Author, Sho Kosugi

Sho Kosugi, one of the best known of all Japanese Martial Artists and actors in the world, grew up as the youngest child and only son of a Tokyo fisherman. At the age of five and a half, he began his Martial Arts training in Shindo- Jinen-Ryu Karate, Kendo, Judo, Iaido, Kobudo, Aikido, and Ninjutsu, and at the age of 18, became the All Japan Karate Champion. At age 19, he left Japan to study and reside in Los Angeles where he earned a Bachelor's Degree in Economics at CSULA.

At the same time, he consistently improved his Martial Arts' skills while learning a wide variety of styles, such as Chinese Xing Yi Quan, Korean Tae Kwon Do, and Japanese Shito-Ryu and Shoto-Kan Ryu Karate.

Throughout the early 1970s, Sho competed in hundreds of Martial Arts tournaments and demonstrations, acquiring more than 660 trophies and medals including consecutive wins of the official City of Los Angeles' Karate Champion titles for 1972, 1973 and 1974.

Mr. Kosugi's film break came 1981 when Karate legend, Mike Stone, contracted with Sho to participate as one of six Ninja Stuntmen in a Cannon Film, titled *Dance of Death*. Soon however, the film's producers and director saw his superb Martial Arts and weapons skills and moved him to a starring role. As the filming progressed it was obvious that he possessed a dynamic screen presence as well and when the picture was released as *Enter the* Ninja, Mr. Kosugi was in a starring role and the rest became history.

Following his film debut, Sho gained an enormous popularity in the '80s and '90s, appearing in more than fifteen motion pictures while starring in more than eleven of them. He was cast in leading and guest starring roles in many episodic television shows including *The Master* with late Lee Van Cleef. Mr. Kosugi's captivating screen presence assured him of a unique place in the history of Martial Arts' Cinema. In 2009, a costarring role in Ninja Assassin, earned him considerable praise and critical acclaim.

Sho Kosugi, the father of actors, Kane and Shane Kosugi, remains active in Martial Arts and today's Hollywood Film industry.

Lightning Source UK Ltd.
Milton Keynes UK
UKHW020616280619
345213UK00012B/438/P